Halvar Was Shocked Awake By A Blast Of Cold Air.

He rolled off the pallet, stiff and achy, to find a pair of boots looming over him.

Hands heaved him to his feet. It was Flores his face a mask of chagrin.

"Bad news, Capitán," he stated. "We've found another one."

"Another what?"

Halvar ran a hand through his hair and scratched the stubble on his chin. He wanted the latrine, the *hammam* and a barber, and mokka, not necessarily in that order.

"Body," Flores said, handing him his clothes.

Halvar hauled his breeches over his braies and shrugged into his coat. He looked for his two caps. Both had served well to protect his head from blows. He felt naked without them.

"Whose body"

"Long Liz."

That got Halvar's attention.

Also By Roberta Rogow

Murders in Manatas
Mischief in Manatas
Mayhem in Manatas

MENACE
in
MANATAS

The Saga Of Halvar
The Hireling
Book 4

Roberta Rogow

This book is a work of fiction. Names, characters, places and incidents are products of the author's imagination or are used fictitiously. Any resemblance to actual persons or events is purely coincidental.

MENACE IN MANATAS

© 2016 by Roberta Rogow

ISBN 978-1-61271-315-1

Cover art and design © William Neagle

"Zumaya Otherworlds" and the griffon colophon are trademarks of Zumaya Publications LLC, Austin TX, http://www.zumayapublications.com

Library Of Congress Cataloging-In-Publication Data

Names: Rogow, Roberta, 1942- author.
Title: Menace in Manatas / Roberta Rogow.
Description: Austin, TX : Zumaya Otherworlds, 2016. |
Series: The Saga of
   Halvar the Hireling ; book 4
Identifiers: LCCN 2016013578 | ISBN 9781612713151
(softcover : acid-free
   paper) | ISBN 9781612713175 (epub)
Subjects: | GSAFD: Alternative histories (Fiction) | Mystery fiction.
Classification: LCC PS3568.O492 M46 2016 | DDC 813/.54--dc23
LC record available at https://lccn.loc.gov/2016013578

To My Husband, Murray Rogow
1925 – 2002

I only wish you could have stayed around long enough to see my late-blooming career.

Acknowledgments

Lynne Holdom and Rachel Kadushin helped formulate the Universe of Manatas.

Liz Burton took a chance and published the Saga of Halvar the Hireling.

My thanks to all who made this book possible.

Manatas Town
and Environs

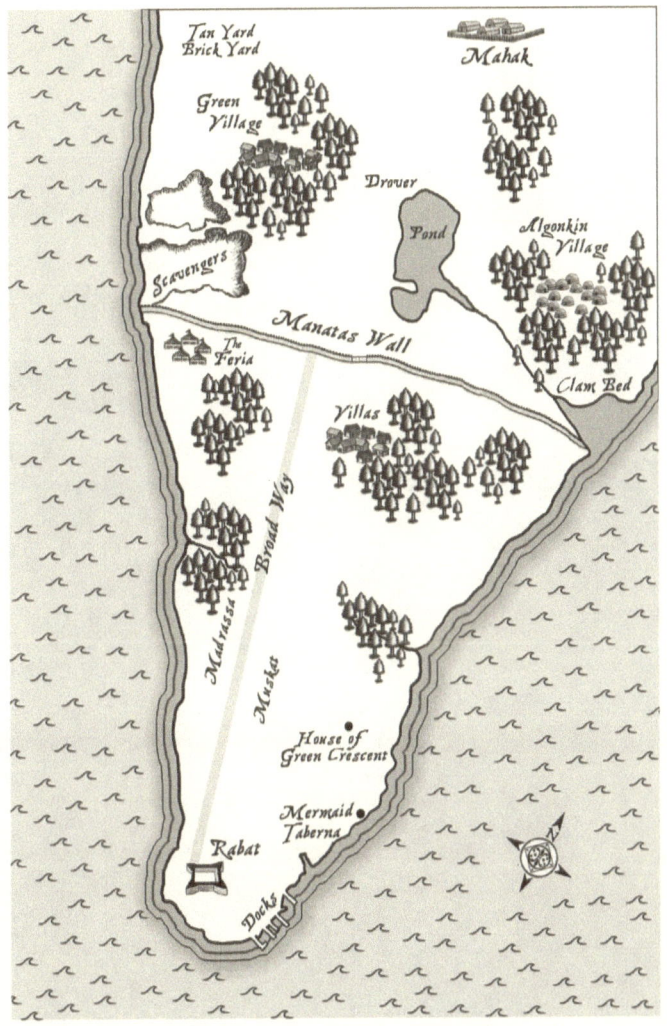

Chapter 1

HALVAR DIDN'T WANT TO BE THE CAPITÁN OF the Town Guards of Manatas. He was not an officer. He had never been in charge of anything. He had been a pikeman in the Free Company of Danes, standing with his fellow pikemen under the watchful eye of Old Sergeant Olaf to hold off the onslaught of enemy troops, until the cannons had decimated the company and he had been left for dead on the field of battle before Pisa.

Then, after Fate, in the form of a zealous battle-nurse, had taken him to Al-Andalus, he'd been a part of the complex network of servants protecting the young man who was heir to the Califate. As the Calif's Hireling, he worked alone.

However, he had been appointed *capitán* by Calif Don Felipe of Al-Andalus-in-Exile, who had told him to keep Manatas safe, and he would do what he had been told to do. He would maintain the Laws of Al-Andalus, laid down by the Prophet in Sharia and the Council and califs of Al-Andalus over the centuries, in this small outpost at the tip of an island in the middle of a river on the coast of a whole new world.

Manatas was the principal trading spot in Nova Mundum, where the Bretain and Franchen merchants from West Caster and Kibbick could meet with the Afrikan providers of kutton, indigo, timber and furs twice a year, at the spring and fall equinoxes. The moon had waxed and waned twice since the buyers and sellers of the Fall Feria had returned to their home ports, leaving the craftspeople from Green Village, the vendors who sold their output in the souk, the students who had come from all over Nova Mundum to learn from the lecturers at the Madrassah, the owners of mokka-shops, and the Local women who cultivated farm plots that served one or the other of these groups to go back to everyday life.

With the itinerant population gone, Halvar found his task easier. There were fewer sailors on the waterfront, and so fewer fights to break up. The students at the Madrassa were intent on their studies for the first weeks of classes, and the mokka-shop debates hadn't gotten to the point of knives being drawn. The god Thor had apparently listened to Halvar's pleas, sending cold drizzle, fog, and wind across the bay, driving the people of Manatas indoors where they could keep their disputes private.

On this day before the longest night of the year, the drizzle had stopped, and a brisk wind was blowing across the bay. Halvar felt confined in his office at the Rabat, previously the domain of the late Tenente Ruíz. The salt breeze blowing in through the small window seemed to urge him to stretch his long legs with another walk around town. The chilly air was refreshing after the heat of summer, and he had purchased a new green coat for winter wear, constructed to order by Yussuf the Tailor, who boasted of his connection to the Calif's Hireling.

Halvar wore his leather-lined cap indoors but the araghoun-fur hat he had bought at the Feria hung on a peg by the door. Baggy breeches and boots completed his outfit, combining the uniform of the Manatas Town Guard with his own common gear. He had been to the *hammam* that very morning to have his twice-a-week shave, and his mustache and hair had been trimmed in anticipation of Yule and the Redeemer's Nativity festivities to come. He was ready to face whatever the Three Old Women wanted to throw at him.

What he currently faced were his immediate subordinates—the three men he had named *tenente* and put in charge of the various sectors that made up the newly-incorporated Manatas Island City, renamed by the calif and the Local sachems in council.

Tenente Flores, the squat Andalusian, had been one of the late Tenente Gomez's staunchest supporters, until the arrival of Halvar and the tumultuous events surrounding the Fall Feria had elevated him from the ranks of Manatas Town Guards. His broad face was pitted with smallpox scars, his bulbous nose had turned red in the wind, and his black beard held, as usual, bits of whatever he'd been eating.

Flores was loyal to Manatas, though, if not Halvar.

Halvar had some reservations about the man's tendency to use force where persuasion might get better results. There were still guardsmen who regarded the Calif's Hireling as an outsider, whose orders they could ignore when they conflicted with what the guards had done in the past. They would obey Flores.

Towering over Flores was Tenente Donal Mac-Donal, the Bretain who had served as constable in Green Village when he was not removing obstreperous patrons from the Gardens of Paradise, the major entertainment hub of Manatas. Donal insisted on wearing his Bretain woolen trews and a smock woven in the Bretain style of checks and stripes Halvar had learned was called a "tartan" with his regulation green coat provided by the Manatas Town Guard commissary.

Under the former administration, Green Village had been a separate entity on the island of Manatas. Following the events of the Fall Feria and the arrival of Don Felipe, Green Village had been made a part of Manatas Island City, and its constabulary had been put under under Capitán Halvar Danske's control. This had not set too well with the Green Villagers, most of whom were Kristo, not Islim, with a few dissident Yehudit. Halvar devoutly hoped that Donal's appointment as *tenente*, and the support of Fru Dani Glick for the merger of the towns, meant that Green Village would no longer be a haven from Sharia and Andalusian justice. As the owner of the Gardens of Paradise, Dani Glick held a unique position in Green Village; without her good-will, Halvar's efforts would be made ten times harder.

The third member of the trio was the Mahak warrior known as Firebrand, the name he had earned by his vehement opposition to Oropan and Andalusian incursions into territory held by Mahak or Algonkin Locals. He scorned the heavy coat and high-crowned *tarboosh* demanded by the Town Guard but had added a fine deerskin *wamus*, or hunting-shirt, and

4

fringed leggings to his usual breech-clout out of respect for the customs of Al-Andalus and as a nod to the increasing chill.

Behind the low desk, notebook open, pen in hand, inkpot open, ready to record what was said, sat Salomey, the daughter of Sultan Petrus, who preferred to go by the name of Selim. Her braids were tucked under a small turban, her ripening figure was swathed in a padded green silk jacket and loose trousers, and she bent to her task with all the fervor of one who has found a calling.

She had decided she would keep the records and act as amanuensis for the otherwise illiterate Capitán Halvar Danske. Sultan Petrus had reluctantly allowed his wayward child to take on this responsibility rather than have her running loose in Manatas getting into trouble. At least, under Halvar's eye, she would be safe from possible danger...or so the sultan hoped.

His three officers currently stood before him, eying one another with suspicion. Each protected his own small bailiwick jealously, each wondered what the sudden changes meant to his own status.

Halvar looked them over. Clearly, one of his jobs would be to get these three to work together. He had no idea how to do it, unless there was some danger that could unite everyone on the island. So far, the only enemy he had seen was the threat of a hard winter, and there was nothing he could do about that.

Instead, he relied on routine. It had worked in the Free Company of Danes. Maybe it would work in Manatas.

"Morning reports. Disturbances? Fights? Burglaries?"

He looked from one *tenente* to the other.

Flores shrugged.

"All is quiet, Capitán. Bad weather keeps folk indoors, so no riots, even after Mullah Abadul's Resting Day sermons. It's Fasting Month, so mokka-shops are closed during the day, by Mullah Abadul's order."

"That doesn't sit well with the Kristos and Yehudit who want their mokka and nibbles," Donal put in. "And the Local women who bake maiz cakes and roast nguba nuts have all gone back to their own villages, so no food in the souk. We all fast, even though we're not not Islim and don't need to."

Flores ignored the interruption and went on with his report.

"Students are too busy with their lessons to get into pointless arguments. No ships in harbor, so no sailors' fights—the whores are complaining about lack of business on Maiden Lane. There are the usual thieves in the souk, but we've let Emir Achmet's two rascals, Osman and Rachev, know we have our eyes on them. Things should pick up soon, once the End-of-Fast feasting starts, but for now, all is quiet."

Donal took up the narration.

"Green Village is preparing for Nativity, nothing to report yet. After the Yule parties get going, and folks start drinking something spicier than mokka, maybe things will get livelier."

"No sign of trouble on the river," Firebrand stated. "My watchmen have seen nothing. But a ship has come into harbor, so perhaps the women in Maiden Lane will stop their complaining. It came with the high tide, when the muezzins called in the *muskats* and the bells in the chapels rang for evening prayers."

Halvar frowned. "I thought all the ships taking goods from the Feria had left."

"There's always the fishing boats," Flores said. "And the mailboat from Bella Mara and Salaamabad arrived this morning. I saw the messenger bringing the packet to the sultan when I came in from my lodgings."

"Not a fishing boat." Firebrand was firm on this point. "And not the dhow that goes along the coast. A round ship. My cousin Muskrat showed it to me when we met last evening. I saw people being rowed ashore. At least four at the oars, three sitting. I think one was a woman, but they all wore capes, so I can't be sure."

"Cargo?" Halvar asked.

Flores stepped into the discussion.

"My man Zoltan didn't tell me about any cargo coming in."

"Would he, if he'd been paid to look the other way?" Donal said with a sneer. "We all know how Gomez worked, turning his back to let extra cargo come ashore for a small 'docking fee'."

"Do you call my men liars and thieves?" Flores's hand flew to the knife at his belt, the same as was carried by every male over the age of thirteen everywhere in the known world.

"Tenente Gomez was known to take a bribe or two," Donal shot back. "Anything to put money into his pocket and take it out of the sultan's."

"What if he did? Anyway, it's not the time for cargo," Flores said. "Whatever that ship is doing, it's not delivering anything that will bring a profit to the calif's treasury."

"Enough of this." Halvar stopped the argument before it went any further. "I'll look into this matter. Whatever this ship is doing here, its captain and crew will have to find lodging and food, and we can question them when we find them. To our other business. Tenente Flores, how goes the recruiting? Anyone ready to join the Manatas Town Guards?"

Flores shrugged again. "We don't even offer as much as Emir Achmet," he said. "All we give is a string of white wumpum every week, a place to sleep and a meal twice a day at the barracks. He's got his own squad in the souk, he's offering one of those shacks he's building against the wall by the pits, plus whatever can be picked up, less his take, of course."

"Of course." Halvar said. "Not much we can do about Emir Achmet. His Scavengers are there to pick up the oddments folks discard, after all. Just keep an eye on those in the souk, make sure they only pick up the discards, and nothing else! Now that the dark days are here, there's more opportunity for those busy fingers to pick things up they shouldn't."

"Don't forget the End-of-Fast festival is coming," Selim reminded him. "And the Yehudit have a festival of their own, where gifts are exchanged. That should make the vendors in the souk happier. And there's their custom of lighting lamps, which will make the candle-sellers happy, too."

"And then there's the Nativity celebration," Halvar added. "Shops will be open late in the souk. Mokkashops on the Broad Way, too, once the End-of-Fast starts. Flores, can you put extra men to watch the souk?"

"I haven't got an army!" Flores complained. "I've only got a dozen, plus Zoltan and Fergus, and they're needed on the waterfront."

"Donal, can you send some of your people into the town?"

Donal's red face grew redder under his auburn beard.

"We've got Yule festivities at the Gardens of Paradise. Things can get a little noisy, especially once they get into the cider and the uskebaugh. And my folk don't like Manatas Town, don't know the place."

"So much the better," Halvar said. "Send two to patrol the Broad Way, keep the students from starting fights over whether Ilha or Chesu will keep a soul from torment in Sheol. Or whether the Earth goes around the Sun, or t'other way around. Or anything else students at Madrassa will argue about."

"Mullah Abadul says it's in the Holy Book—" Flores began, but Halvar cut him off.

"Firebrand, can you spare some of your watchmen to keep an eye on the comings and goings at the waterfront so this Zoltan can be sent to the souk, where he can do more good?"

Firebrand nodded. "I have good warriors, and Sachem Mahmoud sent two Algonkin. Not as good as Mahak, but they will watch the river. Four will keep watch outside Green Village, to see if any of the wolves are hungry enough to hunt near the town. Two more can watch the East Channel. No one will try to sail on the Great River at this time of year—too cold, too much danger. Not even the Huron would dare to attack in winter."

Before Halvar could continue with the next item on his list, a guardsman shoved a Halfling lad in patched coat and trousers into the room.

"What's this?" Halvar snapped. "We're having a meeting here."

"Message from the waterfront," the guardsman announced.

The lad salaamed awkwardly.

"I was sent by Guardsman Zoltan to tell you there is a dead man found on the waterfront, behind Maiden Lane. He asks that someone come quickly and take him away."

"Selim, get Dr. Moise and the dead-cart and follow this lad to the waterfront. Flores, Firebrand, Donal, come with me. You, lad, show us this dead man."

9

Halvar grabbed his fur hat and was out the door before the lad could say any more. At last, he could get out of that office!

Chapter 2

THE MORNING FOG HAD LIFTED, BUT THE AIR
was still chilly when the group left the Rabat, following the Halfling lad through the curving streets that
led to the waterfront district. Halvar settled the fur cap
on his head, grateful for its warmth, aware that his
hairline was receding faster than he would like. Overhead, the sky was bright blue, belying the predictions
of a cold, harsh winter to come.

The lad turned north before they got to the waterfront plaza, leading the party along a narrow path between the blank walls of the warehouses and the back
doors of the small wooden houses on Maiden Lane that
offered lodging and food to temporary visitors, whether
merchants or sailors. They were met by a tall Andalusian Guardsman whose regulation tarboosh added six
inches to his already impressive height. He smoothed
his neatly trimmed mustache with the air of one who
knew just how good-looking he was.

"Guardsman Zoltan," he introduced himself, offering a brisk salaam by way of greeting.

Halvar returned the salute.

"You found this body?"

"Me and Fergus, he's my partner." He indicated the shorter man lurking behind him." "We was doing our rounds, as per orders, checking to see if anyone had tampered with the warehouse locks, and we saw him, just like you see him."

"And sent this lad to fetch us. Good thinking." Halvar turned his attention to the body in question.

It was folded on its knees against the wall of one of the small wooden shacks. Halvar looked right and left and saw only blank walls in either direction. No windows for an interested bystander to peek out of, no one to hear an anguished cry.

Donal and Flores stayed well away from the body, making room in the narrow alley for Dr. Moise and Selim in the donkey cart. Firebrand stepped around the cart to scan the walls and path as the shadows faded back and the sun rose enough to illuminate the stretch of trodden earth.

"We haven't moved him," Halvar assured the slender Afrikan physician.

"Thank you for that," Dr. Moise maneuvered himself alongside the dead man. "Selim, note this—a wound in the back of the neck. Triangular in shape, very small in diameter."

"You think that's what killed him?" Halvar asked.

"I don't think anything yet. It's likely, but we've been mistaken before. I won't know for certain until I've examined him." Dr. Moise beckoned to the two guardsmen. "Come here, you two, and help me move him."

Zoltan and Fergus obediently stepped forward. As they pulled the body away from the wall, the man's head fell back, revealing regular features and a neatly-trimmed beard, pointed in the Franchen style, with a thin mustache. His coat fell open to reveal a fine linen shirt and Franchen-style trousers with the flap hanging open.

Fergus made the sign of the crux.

"'For Chesu's sake, it's Girard!'"

"You know this man?" Halvar asked.

"He came in last spring with that shipload of Afrikans," Fergus explained. "Made an almighty stink, they did. Remember, Zoltan?"

Zoltan shrugged. "Could be. So many ships in and out at feria time, I don't recall them all."

"But this Franchen, he was the one who wouldn't pay Gomez the extra docking fee." Fergus persisted, ignoring the warning looks from both Flores and Zoltan. "Remember? He said he'd been to Manatas before and never had to pay such a fee, and besides, he said, he wasn't docked, he was out in the bay."

Halvar said nothing. This was more proof that the Manatas Town Guard had to be taken in hand by someone scrupulously honest…like himself.

Selim had wrinkled her nose as the body came away from the wall, revealing an odorous stain.

"Couldn't he wait to get to the latrine?" she said with an expressive grimace.

"Guess not," Zoltan said. "The public place is all the way down there." He gestured towards the opening of the alleyway. "Sometimes, you just have to go."

"How long do you think he's been dead?" Halvar asked.

"Not long," Dr. Moise said. "Flesh is cold, but that's understandable. There was frost last night, and it's still chilly."

"When did you two find him?" Halvar turned to Zoltan and Fergus.

"We left the barracks right after dawn prayers." Zoltan answered for both of them. "We must have got here not long after that. Plenty of light to see what was here. Took aback, was Fergus."

"At first, we thought it was one of the Scavengers, or a Local what had took too much fiery-water," Fergus explained. "But then we saw the coat."

"Too fine for a Scavenger, and not the sort the Locals wear," Zoltan added.

"I agree," Halvar said, fingering the material. "This coat's got gold braid on the collar and cuffs, and those are shiny buttons, maybe gold or silver."

"It could still be one of the the Scavengers did it," Donal said. "If it was, all we have to do is find him and get him to the Rabat, and that's that."

"Scavengers wouldn't have left that coat. No, Tenente Donal, this is no mere robbery. Whoever did this meant to kill his victim. The question is, why do it here?"

Halvar looked up then down the alley, to where Firebrand had squatted.

"Tenente Firebrand, what have you found?"

"There is ash here. Someone smoked tabac." Firebrand stood and pointed to a small pile, stirred by the rising wind.

"No footprints," Halvar said. "Ground's too hard."

"I will see if I can find anything else." Firebrand headed towards the end of the alley that led directly to the waterfront plaza.

Selim called out, "There's a passage over here. I think it leads to Maiden Lane."

"Aha! Whores. That's why this fellow was here," Flores said. "He was taking a short break from, ah, important business."

"No one's going to interrupt Long Liz at her work," Zoltan sniggered as they followed the Mahak to his destination. "This is her crib."

14

"How do you know that?" Halvar asked.

Zoltan's handsome face flushed red.

"I patrol the waterfront," he said, his tone stiff. "I know whose crib is whose."

Halvar said nothing.

"These cribs are where the whores take their men," Zoltan continued. "They do their living at other lodgings on Maiden Lane."

"No windows on this side, no peepers," Fergus reported, stating what Halvar had already observed. "Front windows only." He smirked at Donal. "Showing off the goods."

Halvar grimaced in frustration.

"Thor's Hammer! *Someone* must have heard something! Did you two see anyone when you came into this alley? Hear anything?"

Fergus looked at Zoltan, who shook his head.

"It was misty, so we couldn't see nothing. Maybe heard a donkey, all the ways down the alley, at the plaza end."

Firebrand had been walking along the alley, carefully scanning the beaten-earth path.

"Hoy!" he shouted. "Come here!"

When they reached him, he pointed to two ruts in moistened earth where a frozen puddle had recently melted. A small pile of dung still steamed between the marks.

"Someone has been here. Not us. Smaller cart."

"There's your donkey." Halvar thought a bit, then said, "What's the name of that Afrikan halfwit who cleans the waterfront latrine? I see him every morning when I go to the Rabat. He does his rounds regularly. He might have seen or heard something."

"Ibo?" Fergus answered. "You don't think he did this. Never!"

15

"Ibo's harmless," Zoltan agreed. "He picks up the nightsoil from the cribs and the lodging houses, then he cleans the public bog. "

"He must have been through here either just before or just after the crime," Halvar decided. "Tenente Flores, you go back to the Rabat with Dr. Moise and the body. Get your men out, and find this Ibo fellow. I want to talk to him."

"You won't get much out of him," Zoltan said with a shrug. "He can barely speak Arabi, doesn't understand half what he's told."

"He likely saw or heard something," Halvar insisted. "Even if he didn't understand what it was he saw or heard. Tenente, you find him!"

"And what are you going to do?" Donal asked.

"I'm going to have a word with whoever lives in this crib," Halvar said as the donkey-cart moved forward with its sad burden. "Donal, you might as well come along, just in case these women only speak Erse. Firebrand…"

"I stay with you," Firebrand stated. "I was told by my sachem to learn from you how to catch murderers. I will watch how you do it."

"And I'll take notes," Selim said.

Halvar sighed again. He could not control this willful teenager. His only hope was that she would eventually tire of this sordid work and take up another pastime.

In the meanwhile, there was a murderer to catch.

Chapter 3

FLORES CLIMBED UP ON THE CART NEXT TO Dr. Moise, and the grim cortege headed for the Rabat. Halvar and his party squeezed through the narrow passage onto Maiden Lane, a brick-paved street that ran parallel to the East Channel.

There, hastily-constructed wooden houses in the Oropan style jostled Andalusian brick villas. Small passages between each building to provide access to the noisome alley that separated them from the warehouses that held the goods that brought buyers and sellers to Manatas in the first place.

Facing the line of dwellings were a number of small sheds where vendors of fish and vegetables could take shelter during rain or snow showers. The Roumi Rite chapel's bell tower was just visible at the northernmost end of Maiden Lane, with the Kristo burying-ground and the Manatas Town Wall north of that.

Early vendors were making their rounds. A man in a rough kutton jacket led a donkey pulling a cart full of crates of fresh fish. A Local woman in long deerskin skirt and woolen Bretain-style jacket strolled along the street with a basket of esquash, stopping at one or another of the houses to sell her produce to the dwellers therein. Another donkey-cart held lengths of logs, ready to burn in the fireplaces and stoves that kept the inhabitants of Manatas warm during the harsh winter months.

Halvar eyed the nearest shack, built of boards fastened together with wooden pegs, its roof layered with thatch in the Bretain style.

"Is this the one?" he asked Zoltan.

"That's Long Liz Lonergan's crib," the guard confirmed. "She's one of the best on Maiden Lane." He stopped and added, "Or so they tell me."

Halvar nodded. "Of course, you wouldn't know by your own experience."

Zoltan rapped on the door to the crib.

"Long Liz! Open for the Guards!"

"Zoltan, it's too early for collections," a woman shouted from inside. "Come back later for your cut."

Zoltan's face took on a red tinge under his neatly trimmed beard and mustache.

"Liz is a…a friend," he stammered. "We, um, share a meal sometimes."

Halvar said nothing. He understood the relationship between the women who worked the waterfront and the men who were their protectors. If one of his guards acted in that capacity, he would not stand in the way. Of course, he wouldn't make it easy for a guard to take advantage of his position, either. He'd have to consider what to do about Zoltan.

The door flew open to reveal a woman almost as tall as Halvar, her body barely covered by a linen shift under an open kutton robe. Her flaming red hair was a tangle around a face still bearing the signs of the previous night's debauchery.

Halvar tried not to look at the abundant flesh revealed with no effort at modesty.

"I regret to tell you that your, um, client is not coming back."

She looked at the party on her doorstep and fixed her scorn on Zoltan.

"What d'ya mean, not coming back? He's left his gear here, of course he's coming back." She finally appeared to register the significance of the squad standing before her. "Who's this lot?"

Zoltan made hurried introductions.

"This here is Capitán Halvar Danske. And his assistant, Selim ibn Petrus."

"You're the one who got rid of Gomez." Long Liz appraised Halvar with a grin. "Good riddance to that one."

"May we come in?" Halvar asked. "What we have to say is not for the neighbors to hear."

"They'll know soon enough," Fergus said, looking up and down the street. The presence of a squad of Town Guards had people poking their heads out of doors, eager to see what was happening so early in the morning.

Long Liz bowed ironically, with a sweeping gesture that rivaled the play-actors of Bretain.

"Do come in, Capitán Don Alvaro, welcome to my humble abode." She stood aside while Halvar, Zoltan, and Fergus crowded into the room beyond. Donal and Firebrand stayed just outside the door, while Selim hurried in last, tried to find a place to prop her inkpot and notebook and found none.

The single room was lit only by the morning light coming in at the front window. A huge bed dominated it, with two three-legged stools and a small table to one side. Heat came from a brazier of charcoal set under the window, where the smoke could be carried outside by the draft flowing through the house.

Halvar noted a sword and belt hastily thrown on the floor next to the bed. Clearly, the customer had been in a hurry to begin his amorous activities.

Long Liz sat down on the bed, leaving the rest of the group to stand.

"What's this about the captain not coming back? He's left his sword, he's left his purse…"

"We believe we found him behind this house," Halvar said. "About the size of Guardsman Fergus, but slimmer. Dark complexion, small beard and mustache cut in the Franchen style. Wearing a fine coat dyed dark purple, gold lace on the sleeves, gold-looking buttons. Does that sound familiar?"

"*Pie Chesu!*" Liz gasped. "It does sound like Franz. That would be Captain Franz Girard, owner and captain of the *Belle Fleur*," she added proudly. "He always comes to me when he's in Manatas."

"Does he now?" Halvar said. He looked around the room then took a seat on a small stool, studying his surroundings. "Is this where you live, or just where you, um, do business?"

"It's mine," Liz said. "It do get a bit cold in winter, though, so I have a room at La Maison Rouge next door. Fat Gaston lets us women stay there in the winter, when there aren't any sailors to take up space."

Halvar nodded. "This Captain Franz Girard. You say he came to you last night?"

"That he did. I was in Maison Rouge."

"You don't do your, um, business there?"

"It's a taberna, not a brothel," Liz said with a toss of her head. "I don't work a house, I work alone. There's no

20

sailors coming in after the Fall Feria, just a few of the regulars from the Madrassa. Still, they don't appreciate a cold crib, and Fat Gaston don't mind a few extra customers, so long as they don't take up room without they pay for a drink or two."

Halvar nodded. Clearly, the management of whores was more complicated than he thought.

"About this man, this Captain Girard," he said, trying to get back to the reason for their visit. "You say he found you at the Maison Rouge. When was that?"

"Last night, around the time the Holy Meal ended. I was just back from chapel when I saw him and his men coming from the dock. I wasn't expecting him until Spring Feria, but there he was, and right glad to see me he was, too.

"Ask Zoltan—he was there. We was having our evening meal, right after sundown. Up come the captain, fresh from the waterfront, still had the spray on his coat. Said he'd make the usual arrangements. So, we three had our meal, and then we come here, and the captain and me had a fine time."

Zoltan's blush had deepened with each sentence of Liz's blithe recitation.

"It's not what you think…" he began

"What I think is that this dead man is Captain Franz Girard," Halvar said. "And what I want to know is, who killed him, and why was he killed. Have you any ideas on that subject, Fru Liz?"

"He can't be dead," Liz said, desperate. "He's left his gear, his belt, his sword, even his purse. See!" She scrabbled in the pile of oddments at the foot of the bed till she found a small pouch that clinked pleasantly. She shook out a coin and held it out for Halvar's inspection. "He paid for the night, said he'd give me more for Nativity feasting. He said he'd be here until after

Nativity, that he had business with someone in Green Village, and that he'd give me a fine present from the souk."

Halvar frowned as he took the coin and made out the face of Imperator Lovis on the coin and carefully spelled out the inscription. They were written in the Roumi letters that were similar to the Rune he had tried so hard to learn as a lad in the Dane-March.

"Shiny," he commented. He hefted the coin. "Silver, full weight."

"This is new," Selim observed, taking the coin from his hand. "See? It's got the Roumi year—this year—on it. They count from Chesu's Nativity, not from the Prophet's Flight. I think they call these coins 'imperials,' from the inscription of Imperator Lovis."

"What they call these coins doesn't matter. What's important is that Lovis has got his hands on enough silver to mint them." Halvar took the coin back and held it up to the light coming from the small window. "The question is, where did Girard get it, and when?"

Liz stuck her hand out. Halvar gave her back the coin, and she replaced it in the pouch, glaring defiantly at Zoltan.

"That's a gent for you. Don't keep what ain't his." Halvar grinned.

"You keep it, Long Liz. You've earned it."

Liz tucked the pouch under her pillow and leaned back, twitching the coverlet over her lap and folding her arms, daring anyone to take her prize from her.

"What has this to do with the body?" Firebrand asked from just inside the door.

"A good question," Donal said. "Well, Capitán? Now we know who the dead man is, what do we do about it?

"We find out what brought him to Manatas," Halvar said. "Long Liz, what can you tell us about that?"

Liz shrugged, her shift opening over her full breasts.

"I didn't ask. I was just glad to see someone new, that's all. It's been slow since the Fall Feria. I've got a few customers, they come in regular, but Franz was special.

"You know what they say about Franchen? That they love like they cook? Well, Franz must have been one grand cook, 'cause he kept me busy all night long." She smiled happily; then, tears began leaking from her eyes. "You say he's dead? How?"

"A knife in the back of the neck," Zoltan said.

Liz let out a howl and fell back on the bed, kicking the covers aside, her long legs fully revealed.

"He was alive when he left this morning, I swear to you by Chesu and Mother Mara!"

"When *did* he leave?" Halvar asked, trying not to look at the bare legs.

"He'd filled up the pot, had to piss, and went outside just about daybreak," Liz said. "He said he was only going to be a moment, he was coming back for another round." She tossed about on the bed, weeping. "Who would do such a thing? Why?"

"Cover yerself, woman, you're embarrassing the lad!" Donal admonished her, with a glance at Selim.

"Time he learned what his parts is for," Liz replied, but she wiped her eyes, twitched the coverlet back over her legs and propped herself against the wall at the head of the bed.

"Franchen coin, Franchen ship. Girard was Franchen, then," Halvar mused.

"Oh, yes, that he was." Liz took a last shuddering breath and composed herself, pulling the coverlet over her exposed breasts.

"In that case, what was he doing here, in Andalusian waters?" Halvar wondered. "Unless Lovis is now claiming that he rules all the territory once claimed by Al-Andalus, including Nova Mundum…"

He frowned, considering the implications of that idea.

"He didn't say, and I didn't ask," Liz said, wiping her eyes on the coverlet. "We had better things to do than talk politics."

Firebrand poked his head through the doorway, interrupting Halvar's thoughts on international politics.

"There are two women here. They say they have come to speak with Long Liz Lonergan."

"If that's the Islim busybody and her Yehudit pal, I don't want to see them!" Liz called back, pulling the bedclothes around her neck.

"You will answer to us, Fru Lonergan, or be carried to the House of the Green Crescent for examination."

Halvar turned around, startled by the sound of the one voice he'd never have thought to hear on Maiden Lane.

Eva Hakim, the *zyim* of the Manatas Sisters of Fatima, strode into the room in her green hijab and over-robe and brown trousers. She was followed by Dani Glick, proprietress of the Gardens of Paradise, in a snug woolen jacket buttoned to the chin, worn over a full skirt that covered several petticoats. Both women ignored the men and concentrated their attention on Long Liz.

"It is the will of Sultan Petrus and the Town Council of Manatas that all whores must be medically pure," Eva Hakim stated. "To this end, they will submit to our monthly examinations."

"And Old Nokomis of the Mahak is ready to enforce the ruling, Liz," Dani Glick said, "so let's get to it. You've missed the last two months, but this time we've got you. All these men will leave, and we can do what we have to. I get no joy out of it—I've seen enough women's parts to last me a lifetime."

Eva Hakim regarded the males in the room with lofty disdain.

"You may go about your business," she declared.

Dani Glick advanced on the woman cowering in the bedclothes.

"Keep your hands off me, you interfering Yehudit bitch!" Liz snarled.

"That's *Fru* Yehudit Bitch to you, Mistress Lonergan. You would not keep yourself clean at the Gardens of Paradise, but you'll wash yourself now or find somewhere else to do your work. Bos-Town, maybe?"

"Among the Pure Sect?" Liz retorted. "No, Manatas is where I fetched up, Manatas is where I stay."

"In that case, you will comply with the ukase of Sultan Petrus that all women who work on Maiden Lane should be examined," Eva Hakim said sternly. She regarded Fergus and Zoltan with even more distaste. "This is not something men should see. Remove yourselves!"

They left without a further word.

"There's still the matter of a dead man behind this house," Halvar objected. "This woman was the last to see him alive."

"I didn't kill him," Liz cried out. "When he left, I took a nap. I thought I'd need my strength for when he came back."

"He's not coming back now," Donal, who had followed them inside, told her. "Do what you have to, Fru Glick, Eva Hakim."

He and Halvar joined Firebrand in the street, Selim trailing behind them.

"What now?" he asked.

25

Halvar stared at the bay, where a single ship bobbed at anchor.

"If Girard's men lodged at the Maison Rouge, then they should be there still. We'll see if any of them know what brought their captain to Manatas at this time of year."

Chapter 4

LA MAISON ROUGE, THE HOUSE NEXT TO LIZ'S shack on Maiden Lane, no doubt took its name from its redbrick exterior; like most houses on Manatas Island, it was built using a combination of architectural elements. A peaked roof reflected a Danic influence, the brickwork was in the Franchen style, and the narrow windows that faced the street were Andalusian in origin.

"Open up! Town Guard!" Zoltan called as Halvar rapped on the door.

"At this time of day?" grumbled a voice from within. "I paid you last week, Zoltan! Once a month is all I do, you know that."

The door opened to reveal a short, stout man in a Franchen-style coat and striped trousers covered by a stained apron. His round face was gray-stubbled, his eyes narrowed with suspicion under shaggy eyebrows.

His greasy gray hair, tied back with a bit of ribbon, straggled a small embroidered cap.

Zoltan made the necessary introduction.

"Maitre Gaston LeGros, this is Capitán Halvar Danske."

"I know who it is," Gaston snarled. "You're the one did for Tavernier and his wife."

Halvar said, "Tavernier's wife came at me with a poker. I didn't mean to kill her, my arm was pushed. And it was Tenente Ruíz who shot Tavernier, with his pistoia, not me. But that's not why we're here. Let us in, and we'll explain."

"I can't stop you," Gaston admitted, moving aside with a smoldering look at Zoltan and Fergus.

Halvar stepped into the large room that served as the central focus of this combination tavern and lodging house. Square tables with stools were positioned around the side walls. The fireplace on the back wall was flanked by two shelves, one filled with jugs and bottles, the other with an assortment of drinking vessels, some crockery, some metal. Halvar noted the large crux hanging over the fireplace next to a woodcut showing a man sitting on a large chair wearing a crown. Clearly, Imperator Lovis was wasting no time in making himself known to his subjects.

Three men sat on stools, huddled around the fire; two sprawled on benches on either side of the door; and two more emerged from a door that presumably led to the back rooms where travelers could find sleeping arrangements, be they beds or simple pallets on the floor.

Halvar was used to foul odors, and but the stench of the Maison Rouge rivaled that of the notorious sekonk. Odors of boiling cabbage, unwashed bodies, smoldering wood, and stale cider fought for dominance in the smoky room, where something bubbled in a pot hanging on a hook over the fire. Most of the men had clay pipes in their mouths, adding tabac to the collection of aromas.

Donal grimaced as he took in the sordid scene. Selim edged into the room and sat at the table farthest from the fire and the men huddled next to it.

Gaston turned on the last member of the party as Firebrand came through the door.

"Not him!" he declared. "No Locals in my place! Maison Rouge is for Oropans only!"

"And Andalusians, if they can stand the stink of you Franchen," Fergus amended with a sneer of disdain.

"No Locals!" Gaston repeated. "I won't have them here! Outside, you filthy heathen! No redskins here!"

Halvar's jaw clenched. There was a time when he might have had the same prejudice, but his years in Al-Andalus had changed his perception of those with darker skin than his.

"Tenente Firebrand is one of my men," he stated. "He stays with us."

Firebrand sneered.

"I do not need to be in this place. It is not fit for the dogs of the streets to lie in. I will go to the waterfront plaza and find out more about that ship in harbor."

"I'll meet you there," Halvar murmured. "I didn't think this kind of thing went on in Manatas."

"Some Oropans think they own the world. In time, we will remind them that this part of it belongs to Mahak." Firebrand cast another smoldering look at Gaston and slid out the door.

Gaston looked Halvar over with undisguised contempt.

"And what does Capitán Halvar Danske want with me? I'm an honest man, I run a clean place. I obey all

29

of that Islim mullah's stupid rules. No alcohol, no swine's flesh, no forbidden fish. Ask Zoltan!"

Halvar sniffed. He was certain he could distinguish the fatty residue of bacon in the fug, and there was most definitely alcohol being swilled in front of him.

"I don't care whether you serve alcohol, and I'm not here to check your kitchen for forbidden food. I want to know about Captain Franz Girard."

"What about him?" One of the sleepers had raised his head from his bench.

"He's dead," Zoltan announced bluntly.

"What! He was fine last night, got *Belle Fleur* into harbor neat as you please, let us go ashore, and took his meal here last night with his whore and her man." He peered blearily at Zoltan. "You was there, wasn't you?"

Two of the smokers at the fireplace added their voices.

"Long Liz!"

"What a wench!"

A chorus of catcalls and hoots acknowledged the assessment of Long Liz's charms.

"Don't tell me she did for him?" the drunkard exclaimed, managing to sit up. "She's a handful, that one!"

"He didn't die in bed," Zoltan informed him. "We found him in the alley behind the house."

Halvar took over the questioning. He sat down beside the man on the bench.

"Who are you?"

"I'm Michel, called Primero because I'm the number-one mate on *Belle Fleur*. What's this about Captain Girard being found dead behind this house?" He turned to Gaston. "Bring me a glass of cider, I need a drink!"

"Looks like you've had enough," Halvar commented.

"Hair of the dog," Michel mumbled. "Just to clear my head."

Halvar beckoned Selim over.

"Take notes," he said. "This might be important."

Selim sat, pen and notebook in hand, her eyes wide as she surveyed the sordid scene.

"How can people live like this?" she muttered.

"I've seen worse," Halvar murmured back.

Donal moved closer to Zoltan and Fergus. Michel eagerly gulped down the raw liquid provided by the landlord.

"Ooof!" he grunted. "That stuff's strong!"

"Alcohol is forbidden in Manatas Town," Halvar said, with a glance at Gaston.

Donal shrugged. "You see how it is. The folk on the waterfront don't want to go all the way to Green Village for a drink of something stronger than mokka. Gomez used to look the other way, if he was given enough wumpum or silver to do it."

"Just as long as they don't sell it to Locals," Zoltan said. "They go mad with it. That's why Maitre Gaston won't have them in his place, nor will most of the other tabernas on the waterfront."

Michel coughed, drawing Halvar's attention away from the prejudices of Oropans in Manatas and back to the matter at hand.

"Tell me about Captain Girard," Halvar said in halting Franchen.

"I can speak better Franchen," Selim piped up. "You can talk to me, Michel Primero, and I'll tell the capitán what you said."

"I know Arabi," Michel said. "I'll speak for myself." He took another swallow of Gaston's raw cider and switched to that language. "We wasn't supposed to be here this trip. We was supposed to take our passengers to the new city Sultan Calavera is building, the one he calls Bella Mara, after Mother Mara. It's a fancy of his, him being Roumi Rite, that Mother Mara is his patron—he's even named his territory after her. Calls it Terra Mara instead of using the Local name Powhatan."

"Passengers? At this time of year?" Halvar tugged at his mustache to aid in his thought processes. "Not a good time for travel, it's almost winter."

"True, true," Michel agreed. "And we was almost ready to winter in Kibbick, but then this Bretain milord comes along with a bag full of silver and says we must take him and his woman and their two servants to Terra Mara. And the captain, he takes the silver, puts the passengers in the good cabins, and off we goes."

"And when was this?" Halvar did some mental calculations. He'd arrived in Manatas shortly after the Fall Equinox, two months before. It took some time to sail from Kibbick south to Manatas, with the current and wind urging the ships north and east, back to Oropa, instead of south and west towards Nova Mundum.

"I think the first ships was coming in from the Fall Feria when we set out," Michel said, after another swig of cider. "And we had to put in at Bos-town for supplies, and there was some trouble about Milord Summersby and his lady the captain had to put right before we could go on our way."

"These passengers…what was their reason for sailing at this time of year?"

"Not my concern." Michel shrugged. "I don't want nothing to do with passengers. I told that to the captain when he first put them aboard. He says to me, 'You steer the ship, Michel. Leave the rest to me." So I did, and much good it did him."

Halvar stifled his impatience, and let the man ramble between swigs of cider.

"First, we take Afrikans from Savana port. Then, it's the Franchen, back to Franchenland. Then it's a shipload of women. And then, that Milord and his man and the woman and her maid, which I know what she is, and it ain't a maid. I sail the ship, I follow the course Captain Girard lays out, see that the bosun keeps the men in order. That's my work.

"I don't like passengers, especially women. They're bad luck, and more bother than they're worth, no matter how much silver gets thrown about."

"And yet you had them on board," Halvar said.

"We did. First the Afrikan and his wives and all their servants, then the lot from Franchenland to Kibbick, and finally that Milady and the old woman with her, what was on the ship when we was sailing from Franchenland.

"And all of them yorking their heads off, and yelling for Chesu or Mother Mara to ease their pain. Except for the ones that had stronger stomachs, and they were moping about the food, or chasing my men. Captain Girard was paid well for all his trouble, and made sure we got our share, but those women weren't worth the silver, if you ask me."

Halvar smirked in spite of himself. He was an excellent sailor, but he had spent his voyage across the Storm Sea in the company of a frater who suffered mightily from the excessive pitching and yawing of a fast dhow. The so-called round ships, those newfangled fluyts and galleons, were built to be more stable than a dhow but less speedy, sacrificing swiftness for expanded cargo room. The sea still rolled, and so did the ships on the waters.

"These passengers you brought here, this Milord and Milady Summersby," Halvar said. "Where are they now? Are they here?"

He looked around the room again. Michel let out a squawk of derisive laughter.

"Catch them at a place like this? When we anchored, Milord asked where they could find proper lodgings, if we had to be here for a while. Captain Girard told them about the Mermaid Taberna, said it was run by a respectable Franchen and his wife, who had a large set of rooms to let. Once they was ashore, he took Milord and Milady there.

"Only Gaston told me the old landlord and his woman got killed, and some Danic pirate is running the place now. Girard left them with the bodyguard, that old soldier who came with us from Franchenland, and joined us here at Maison Rouge."

"Where he met Long Liz?" Halvar hinted

Michel grinned. "She was here, warming her bottom, and she lit up like a Nativity lantern when she saw him."

"Girard didn't know about Hannes Zilberstanm," Halvar muttered to Donal.

"I don't suppose word's got to Bos-Town or Kibbick there's been a change of ownership at the Mermaid," Donal said. "It takes a while for news to reach places not in Andalusian territory, and if this Girard had been at sea, he may not have heard what happened at the Fall Feria."

"Not even if they got the *Gazetta*?" Selim wondered. She was proud of her friends' efforts in establishing a regularly published news-sheet in Manatas.

"The *Gazetta* doesn't get sent as far as Bos-Town, let alone Kibbick," Halvar pointed out. He turned back to Michel. "Tell me about Captain Girard. What sort of man was he? Was he the kind who makes enemies? Starts quarrels? Flirts with other men's women?"

"Ah! Women!" Michel nodded sagely. "That was the captain's other weakness. Money was the first—he'd do most anything, sail anywheres, if the reward was big enough. And he liked the women, that's for sure, the bigger the better. Oh, he was polite to Milady whenever she poked her head out of that cabin for a breath of air. But she wasn't to his taste—too dainty, ye see.

"He liked 'em big, like Long Liz. He'd had her when we came in last spring, when we brought the Afrikans north from Savana Port. He liked that kind, he said, because he could dig deep! Haw!"

Selim bent over her book to hide her embarrassed flush. Donal grinned; Zoltan and Fergus joined in the sailor's raucous laughter.

Halvar considered this information.

"Aside from his liking for large women and easy money, what else can you tell me about Captain Girard? Why did he put into Manatas when he was supposed to sail south to Terra Mara?"

Michel looked into his tankard, found it was dry, and beckoned for a refill.

"What can I tell you? Like I told you, Captain Girard was a canny man, with a good eye for a bargain. He owned his own ship, d'ye see, so he could take on whatever cargo came our way.

"We sailed out of Savana Port in spring, got here in time for the Spring Feria. Then across the Storm Sea, got to port in Junius. Back across the Storm Sea to Kibbick—that got us there at the fall tides.

"He was going to take the winter to refurbish the ship, but he couldn't resist those silver imperials, so off we sail again, heading south. We put in at Bos-town for supplies. There was the trouble about Milady Summersby, which he got that squared away, and off we go again, down the coast, with the captain checking the charts all the way until we got around the Long Island.

"That's when he told me to head into Manatas Bay. He felt a storm coming, and he wanted to be out of its way."

"Weather-wise, was he?"

"Indeed, he was! Could feel a storm in his bones, as they say. Saved our lives more than once." Michel accepted another tankard of cider. "But there may have been more to it. He spent a good deal of time ashore at Bos-Town, conferring with some of their merchants. And before he went off with Long Liz, he sent a message to some merchant. I don't know what it was about or who this merchant is. Like I say, I left the business to the captain. I sailed the ship, to his orders."

Halvar digested this information.

"Have you any idea as to who might have wanted to kill him?"

Michel shook his head.

"Not here in Manatas. Maybe back in Franchenland, if he'd run afoul of some husband, but that's not likely, is it? I mean, why come all the ways here? We wasn't even supposed to be here!"

"But Captain Girard is dead, all the same," Donal said. "He must have had an enemy somewhere."

"What about the other men on board ship?" Halvar pressed on. "Was Captain Girard a harsh sailing-master? Did he have any enemies among the crew?"

"Not our men," Michel said. "There are some captains leave everything to the sailing-master, I don't deny it, because I've sailed with them. But not Girard. He kept the ship in order, made sure we got our pay, kept a good galley, put in for supplies, didn't stint on the food like some do. Even had a barrel of sweet apples aboard, said it kept away the scurvy, and maybe it did, because I sailed five years with him, back and forth from Oropa to Afrika and up and down the coast of Nova Mundum, and nary a bit of scurvy did we get.

"I hope you catch whoever did this, Capitán, because he took the life of one of the best men I've ever

36

known. Captain kept me sober as long as we was at sea, and let me go when we was ashore, and you can't say better of any man." Michel stood up and raised his mug out toward the crux. "May he rest in the arms of Chesu and Mother Mara." He sat down again. "Where is he now?"

"On his way to the Rabat, to be examined by our doctor."

"What for? He's dead, ain't he?"

"Dr. Moise is an expert at finding out what kills people," Selim explained.

Michel thought this over, then nodded.

"You find who did it, you tell me. I'll send him to Sheol!"

"No, you won't," Halvar told him. "When we find this murderer, he'll face the sultan at the next Grand Divan, after the Spring Feria."

"And what about Captain Girard? What will you do with him?"

"I suppose, being Franchen, Girard followed Roumi Rite." Halvar turned to Donal. "Is there a place for sailors at the Roumi Rite burying-ground?"

"Not in the ground," Michel interrupted. "When you are finished with him, give him to us, his crew. We'll take him to his proper rest at sea, where he spent his days. I can steer *Belle Fleur* well enough, once I've got the way plotted."

"But you'll need charts," Halvar mused. "Where were Girard's charts, his maps, his logbooks?"

"Back aboard, I suppose," Michel said. "No need to take them ashore with him, is there?" He finished the last of his drink. "I'd better find a proper prester, see to the captain's funeral."

"Down the end of Maiden Lane." Donal gave the directions. "Ask for Prester Nicodemus."

Gaston LeGros had hovered near the group. Now, he approached with a tray of crockery mugs.

"May I serve the guards with some sweet cider? No alcohol."

"Another time," Halvar said. "Michel Primero, you and your men must stay in Manatas until this matter is finished. Try not to kill each other while you're here. And as soon as you're sober enough to walk, go to the Rabat and ask to see Dr. Moise. I want to verify that the dead man is Captain Girard."

With that, he, Donal and Selim left the first mate and crew of the *Belle Fleur* to their drinking and smoking.

As they returned to the waterfront plaza, Halvar considered what he'd learned. If Girard was a womanizer, perhaps he'd provoked this Milord Summersby by being too friendly with Milady. But why wait until now, and why do it in Manatas?

The answers, he believed, lay with those mysterious passengers, and Halvar hoped they would be found at the Mermaid Taberna.

Chapter 5

BY THE TIME HALVAR AND HIS PARTY ARrived the waterfront plaza, the morning mist had cleared. Two small dinghies bobbed at one end the dock, off-loading their cargoes of fish and vegetables; the first had been caught in the waters around Manatas Island, the other brought in from the farms on the Round Island across the bay.

A slender dhow, sails furled tight against its spars, was tied to the other side of the dock. Andalusian women swathed in heavy robes, their faces veiled, bargained for the produce, while Local women leading large dogs hitched to three-pronged frames fought with them for the choicest fish. When they'd filled their baskets, the Andalusians headed back to their homes, while the Locals set off towards the Broad Way to sell their wares to those who could not or would not go to the waterfront themselves.

Gulls wheeled overhead, adding their raucous cries to those of the fishermen and vegetable-sellers. Feral cats prowled around the crates and baskets, hoping to snatch a mouthful of fish-offal. Over it all hung the smell of fish and saltwater.

Halvar ignored the scene, which had become familiar in the weeks he'd spent in Manatas. Instead, he headed straight across the plaza to the focal point of social life on the waterfront and his temporary home on the island—the two-story building called the Mermaid Taberna.

Then, the tall Dane stopped in mid-stride to gaze at the tall ship in the middle of the bay.

"That must be *Belle Fleur*," he said.

"So it must," Donal agreed. "What of it?"

"I've got to get to it." Halvar frowned "Where are the barges? Where are the skiffs and dinghies that take the crews and cargoes ashore?"

"Beached," Zoltan said. "No need for them after the Fall Feria. The small boats and narrow dhows can sail into the East Channel and dock. It's only the round ships, those galleons and fluyts, that can't risk running aground on the rocks around some of those small islands in the bay. They anchor farther out, away from the tricky currents."

"Ah." Halvar's frown deepened. "Then how did Girard get ashore?"

Firebrand pointed to a small rowboat tied at the end of one pier.

"That must be the dinghy from the ship."

"I suppose we can use that," Halvar said. "Zoltan, you and Fergus find some men to row it and meet me here after the muezzin calls for mid-morning prayer. I'll go to the Mermaid Taberna. Our genial host Hannes Zilberstam may be able to tell us more about Captain Franz Girard and his passengers."

Firebrand looked across the bay.

"I will get us to the ship," he announced. Then, he strode swiftly back down Maiden Lane, leaving Halvar to herd Donal and Selim into the taberna.

Halvar entered the central room of the Mermaid Taberna and sniffed the air expectantly. Once Hannes Zilberstam had been confirmed in his position as rightful proprietor he had taken steps to improve the taberna's appearance and cuisine. He had hired a Danic widow to provide meals that would satisfy the Oropan need for hearty food free of the peppers and spices that rendered Andalusian and Afrikan dishes unpalatable to Franchen, Danic, Bretain and Scanian tongues and stomachs. Fru Marta was already busy in the kitchen, preparing the hearty soup and black bread that would be served at midday.

Halvar noted some new additions to the otherwise sparse décor. The servers were busily placing boughs of pine across the wide mantel of the fireplace. More greenery was being nailed around the front windows that let only a little light into the dark interior.

"Preparing for Yule, Hannes Zilberstam?"

Hannes stumped forward to greet his most prominent tenant.

"That I am. The All-Father be praised that we'll get through the dark days and into the sunlight again when the spring comes. You're back early, Capitán. I didn't expect you until after sundown."

"I'm not here for pleasure, Heer Zilberstam. Have you heard the news yet? The body of Captain Franz Girard was found behind one of the cribs in Maiden lane."

Hannes's wide grin turned into a worried frown.

"I hadn't heard. The news-crier hasn't spread that word yet."

"He will. Before he does, I have to know what you can tell me about this Girard." Halvar sat down at one of the tables lined up against the side wall.. "And bring mokka for me and my men."

Hannes beckoned to one of the Halfling servers, who vanished into the kitchen and emerged a few minutes later carrying a tray laden with a brass ewer and crockery mugs. Donal sat the bench on one side of Halvar, Selim on the other, notebook and inkpot ready.

"What can I tell you? Not much." Hannes sat on the chair across the table from Halvar, his wooden leg protruding from his loose trousers. "I never met the man until yesterday."

"For one thing, you can tell me when Captain Girard arrived. He wasn't in here last night when I came from the Rabat for my dinner. And I didn't see any new faces when I played at tables, either."

Hannes grinned slyly. "Looking for someone else to rook, are you? Not Girard, he's Franchen, too clever for a Dane." He closed his eyes in thought then opened them. "Girard and his people came between mid-afternoon and dusk prayers. Him and his passengers, looking for the Taverniers."

"Whom they didn't find," Selim said.

"And much put out about it they were," Hannes said. "I told them the Mermaid was under new management, but I could accommodate them with quarters, of a sort, for a small rental fee."

"Not *my* rooms!" Halvar exclaimed.

He had appropriated two upstairs rooms carved from a storage attic and previously occupied by the painter-turned-frater Leon di Vicenza. He had spent one of his precious hoard of gold pieces on furnishings from the souk—two extra stools and a cloth drape to hang in the doorway that separated his eating-quarters from his sleeping-room. He had even gone so far as to place a small crux and a picture of Chesu and Mother Mara on the shelf where Leon had stacked his books. It was the first time in his life that he'd a place of his own, and he would not give it up to some passing Bretain milord!

"Not at all, not at all," Hannes assured him. "Those rooms are yours, Capitán! But that house of the Taverniers, it's been standing unused since I got it."

"A fine brick house, not being used?" Donal considered his mug of mokka, took a sip, and made a grimace of distaste. "What do you put in this stuff, bilge from the ships?"

"Chicory leaves," Hannes said. "It makes the mokka-beans last longer. And as for that house, I spent one night in it, and that was enough to make me head back to my cubby under the stairs here at the taberna. Have you seen it? It's full of images, the most disgusting stuff! Like living in a torture chamber, it was!"

Halvar recalled the paintings of the Redeemer on his crux, and the holy men and women being martyred.

"Not the most cheerful thing to see before bedtime," he agreed.

"And by the time I got there, those thieving Scavengers had lifted everything moveable from the kitchen, all the pots and pans and crockery," Hannes went on, more aggrieved by the minute. "The only things left were the big table and chairs from the front room, and the beds in the chambers up the stairs, and the only reason they didn't take them was because they were too heavy for one person to carry, and they didn't have a cart to haul them off with them."

"In that case, why rent the house to these gentry?" Halvar asked.

"Girard's passengers? They wanted room for four, and there was room for four in that house," Hannes replied. "So, I sent them over there—the Bretain Milord Henry Summersby and his Franchen Milady, and their servants, with one of my lads to settle them in.

"Then, that manservant comes trotting back with the Franchen soldier who calls himself a bodyguard, and the woman what calls herself Dame Brigitte, demanding that we give them household goods, coverings for the bed, draperies for the windows, crockery to eat off off, cutlery to eat with, all that stuff. I found some extra crockery and cutlery in the storeroom, but no draperies or any of that nonsense.

"Then they demanded a basket of food. I invited them to take their meal here, but no! The Mermaid Taberna's a low place, not fine enough for Milord and Milady, according to that sniffy servant."

Halvar sipped his mokka thoughtfully. He was getting used to the bitter tang of the chicory.

"Bretain, you said? And who is this bodyguard?"

"The serving man was one of those Bretains looks down his long nose at the rest of the world. The woman was Franchen, had a mouth on her, ranted at Fru Marta, said the food wasn't fine enough for her milady.

"As as for that bodyguard, he was a right rascal. I've seen his like before. Old soldier, I'd say. Swaggered about in high-heeled boots, sword at his hip, pistoia in his belt. He was the only one had any Arabi, the others spoke only Franchen and some Erse. And they treated this fine taberna like some low dive!"

"Whereas it's the grandest place on Manatas," Donal put in. "Excepting the Gardens of Paradise."

"There's some that don't care to go all the ways to Green Village for a decent meal and an evening of fun." Hannes retorted, stung by the implication his establishment was the lesser attraction.

"Which you provide by stealing our entertainers."

"I offered Willem of Cos a wage instead of making him live off whatever he could pick up as a gratuity," Hannes retorted. "Of course he came to me! If you want him back, pay him what he's worth. And I don't have to have naked girls to attract customers—Fru Marta's cooking does it for me."

Halvar interrupted before the argument got personal.

"What was your impression of Girard? Did any of the regular customers here know him? Do you think he had any enemies here in Manatas who might have had it in for him?"

Hannes thought for a moment.

"There was that Afrikan captain out of Savana Port, but he's long gone. I wasn't here before the Fall Feria, so I wouldn't know of any enemies he might have had when the Taverniers ran the place. As for those passengers, the Bretain Milord and the Franchen Milady... there's something odd about them, but I can't rightly put my finger on it. It'll come to me."

Halvar took out his string of wumpum. Hannes waved his hands in negation.

"Not for you, Capitán."

"Put the mokka on my bill," Halvar ordered. He turned to Selim. "You get back to the Rabat. Inform the news-criers what has happened, tell them to spread the word that we're looking for anyone with information about Captain Franz Girard."

"What about that Bretain Milord?" Donal asked.

"I'll deal with him later. You find those servants, talk to them in Erse. If they don't know Arabi, they may open up to someone who speaks their language."

"And what are you going to do?"

"I'm going to get the boat and find out what's happening on that round ship in the harbor."

Chapter 6

THE BREEZE HAD BECOME STRONGER BY THE time Halvar, Donal, and Selim left the Mermaid Taberna. The ripples on the bay had white caps, and the waves lapped harder at the wooden logs that held the plank piers of the docks in place.

Halvar looked over the waves to the ship bobbing in the middle of the bay, anchored between two of the small islands that attracted seabirds to Manatas.

"What now?" Selim asked. "I know—I'm supposed to go back to the Rabat." She started to pout. "You may need me on that ship."

"There's something else I want you to do, laddie. And don't pout at me, because you're the only one can do it."

Selim's eyebrows stopped in mid-frown.

"Me?"

"Yes, Selim. I can't read or write Arabi—you can. They keep records of ships going in and out of port, don't they? To keep track of the calif's tolls, and how much cargo comes in and out?" Halvar thought aloud.

"And you want me to find out when that ship, *Belle Fleur*, last came to Manatas," Selim said.

"Clever lad!" Halvar said, patting her shoulder. "Captains have to report to the tallymen when they come into port. There will be some record of the ship, where she came from, and where she was bound. If she carried cargo, what it was, and if she carried passengers, who they were. Anything to do with Girard or his ship."

Donal tried to follow Halvar's reasoning.

"Why ask about the ship? He wasn't killed there, he was killed here."

"But he wasn't expected to make port here," Halvar reminded him. "According to Primero, they were headed south, to Bella Mara in Terra Mara. He only put in here because he thought there was a storm brewing. No one knew he was coming here, as far as we know, and he thought he'd find a safe haven with other Franchen, the Taverniers."

"Who spied for Imperator Lovis," Selim pointed out. "Was Girard also a spy? Maybe he had information for them, and their two assassins."

"Who are also dead," Halvar finished the tally. "But Girard is dead, too, so we can only guess why he decided suddenly to come to Manatas. Maybe I'll find out something on the ship, a journal or some papers, that will tell us why he came here."

"If he thought he'd find safe haven here, he was mistaken," Donal said. "The Franchen in Green Village are mostly the ones who were running from Lovis, not the ones who favor him. For all we know, one of them could have had it in for Girard."

"But he didn't go anywhere near Green Village," Selim objected. "He went directly to the Mermaid Tab-

47

erna, and when he didn't find Franchen there, he went to Maison Rouge."

"He sent a message to some merchant," Donal reminded Halvar.

"It can't have been pressing, because he found Long Liz and spent the night carousing with her." Halvar said.

"So, the only ones who knew he was here were his own people." Donal said. "His own crew, the Bretains, and their servants and the bodyguard."

"And whoever he sent the message to," Selim said. "We have to find out who carried that message, and who got it."

"If they did get it," Halvar said. "I'll have Flores put his men on it."

"What am I supposed to say to ask the Bretains?" Donal asked.

Halvar sighed inwardly. Donal knew how to stop a fight and how to nab a thief. Subterfuge was beyond him.

"Tell them you're with the Town Guard, that you've found Captain Girard dead, and that the Bretain Milord and Milady will be stranded here on Manatas until we are satisfied that neither of them had anything to do with his death. You can be a straightforward as you like."

"What if Milord won't speak to me?" Donal looked worried. "High in the instep, these milords. Don't talk to just anyone."

"Then tell the servants that if they won't speak to you, the Capitán of Guards—that's me—will be along presently, and that I will see Milord Summersby whether he wants to see me or not. Don't tell them exactly how or where Girard died, just that he was found dead by the Town Guardsmen. I want to lay a few traps for Milord and Milady, and especially that bodyguard. If he's an old soldier, it's possible I know him or, at least, know his company."

Donal salaamed and set his tarboosh straight. Selim looked at the increasingly rough water and decided that, for once, she would do as she was ordered.

Before they could leave the waterfront, Firebrand appeared suddenly, as was his custom, this time popping up the ladder that led from the pier to the water.

"I have a canoe," he announced. "We can go to the round ship now."

Donal's apprehensive frown relaxed into a grin.

"There's your boat, Capitán," he said

Halvar looked down at his transport. A long, narrow object held two Locals in hunting shirts and leggings, each bearing a paddle. One had the distinctive shaven skull and scalplock of the Mahak, the other wore his hair in two braids, held in place by a leather strap. The boat, such as it was, was made of bark stretched over a wooden frame. It looked barely capable of carrying the two paddlers, let alone two more passengers.

Halvar stared dubiously at the canoe.

"Are you sure this will hold me?"

"I have taken many beaver skins across this water in canoes," Firebrand assured him. "Muskrat is my cousin. Seulemon and he are the best paddlers on the river. Together, they have won many times at the Spring and Fall Feria races.

"We can get across to the round boat while the tide is going out, finish our business there, and ride the tide back. Just be careful how you sit. You must not move too hard, or you will tip the canoe."

Selim and Donal watched with malicious grins as Halvar eased himself into the unsteady vessel, fold-

49

ing his long legs under his bottom so that the heels of his boots pressed uncomfortably into his buttocks. He gripped the sides of the canoe and sent a quick plea to the Redeemer for assistance. After all, the Redeemer was supposed to have been friendly with fishermen, and had walked on the surface of a sea.

He shouted over his shoulder, before the canoe left the dock, "Tenente Donal, see that Selim gets to the shipping office. Then find those servants. I'll be back by midday."

He didn't dare look back to see if his orders had been obeyed; he fixed his eyes on the ship in the harbor. As Firebrand found his place in the bow of the canoe, Muskrat let go of the rope that held the canoe to the dock, and they were off.

Halvar had always considered himself a good sailor. He had spent time during his youth in the Dane-march on his uncle's fishing boat, an experience that had made him all the more eager to join the Danish Free Company when the opportunity presented itself. He had endured two long sea voyages, one from Italia to Al-Andalus and one across the Storm Sea from Al-Andalus to Nova Mundum, and he had never felt the pangs of *mal-de-mer*.

Now, bouncing along the choppy waves of Man-atas Bay in this fragile craft made him more forgiving of those who had suffered. His stomach seemed to rise and fall with every dip and swell. He was horribly aware of the distance between himself and dry land. Spray from the rising waves dampened his woolen coat and coated his mustache with salt.

He was almost ready to order the canoe to turn back when he realized the wooden hull of the *Belle Fleur* was in front of him. The sides of the ship bowed out above the tiny canoe as they padded around looking for a point of access. The ship's rudder offered no hand-holds; the anchor chain was taut but slick with spray, too risky even for a good climber. Halvar didn't think he could do it in his boots, even if Firebrand's macassin could manage the footholds.

"Hoy! Ahoy the ship!" he called, first in Arabi, them in Erse, then in Danic. That used up his linguistic accomplishments.

There was no answer.

"Are there no sailors on board?" Firebrand asked.

"Strange. No captain will leave his ship unattended in port," Halvar said. "Aha! Ladder!"

A rope ladder dangled from a gap in the rails overhead. There was a considerable distance between the last rung and the canoe. Halvar stood up, feet planted firmly apart, arms stretching until the tips of his fingers reached the slat that formed the bottom rung of the flimsy ladder.

While the paddlers strained to keep the canoe steady, he rose on tiptoe so he could hook his fingers around the wooden slat. The canoe slid away, leaving him dangling by the ladder, swinging over the surging waves. With a mighty effort, he hauled himself up until he could get his arm around the slat and brace his feet against the ship's side. Then he grabbed the ropes forming the sides of the ladder, rough and slick with salt, and called down, not daring to turn his head,

"Firebrand, tell your men to tie onto the anchor chain and wait for us. I'll go up and see what's happening."

Halvar heaved himself rung by rung, bracing his feet against the planks of the ship's hull. Inch by inch he rose, until, after mounting the first three rungs, he managed to hook his boot-heels onto the flimsy rope ladder. He heard ominous creaks and hoped it would bear his weight. He forced himself not to look down into the cold dark depths of the bay beneath him.

He felt a twitch on the ladder just as he reached the ship's rail. He clutched at a stanchion as he lifted himself over the gunwale of the ship and fell onto the deck. Firebrand followed him more gracefully.

"I thought I told you to stay in that canoe," Halvar said, scrambling to his feet.

"You may need help." The Mahak looked around the deck. "I thought these round ships were full of sailors. Who puts up the sails, ties all the ropes?"

No one was in sight. The sails were neatly furled against the spars, the masts secured with guy-ropes, but those who had done the work were elsewhere.

"Ahoy the ship! We are from Manatas Island!" Halvar called out again. Again, there was no answer.

"What do we do now, Dane?" Firebrand asked.

"We find out what Captain Girard was up to in Manatas." Halvar straightened his coat, set his fur cap firmly on his head, and prepared to search for answers.

Chapter 7

HALVAR HAD BEEN ON THE SCHOONERS THAT plied the waters between the Dane-march and Scania. He had been on the dhows that crossed both the inner and outer seas ruled by Al-Andalus and its allies in Afrika. He had heard about the newfangled fluyts, the "round ships" so called because they had been constructed so the cargo holds were wider than the decks above them, but he had never been on one.

Belle Fleur clearly belonged to this class of ship. It was considerably larger than a schooner, wider than a dhow, with two masts towering over her deck. The ship was well cared for. All ropes had been properly secured. The deck was clear of trash, showing good management. The ropes that held the masts in place were neatly tied, no loose ends to trip the unwary sailor. Whatever else Captain Girard had done, he ran a tight ship.

Once more Halvar called out, first in Arabi, then in Danic, finally in Erse: "Halloo! We are from Manatas! By order of the Sultan, we board this vessel!"

Once again, no answer.

Firebranch cocked his head towards the bow.

"Someone is singing," he remarked. "They don't hear us."

"We've announced ourselves. Not our fault if they don't listen."

Halvar headed for the stern, the place most likely to hold the captain's personal quarters, close to the helmsman at the ship's rudder. Sure enough, there was a flimsy shed built around the long bar by which the ship was steered. A hatch and ladder in front of the shed led to the middle deck. Halvar eased down the ladder, where he was confronted with a small passageway and three closed doors.

"Captain's cabin," he pronounced, tapping the door at the end of the small corridor. It opened to reveal a single room that spanned the width of the ship, with a bunk bed built against the bulkhead under the small window at the flat end of the ship. A round table was fixed to the deck in the middle of the cabin. Cabinets built into the bulkheads held drawers, all latched so that the contents could not spill out as the ship rolled in the swell.

One shelf held a sextant and a spyglass. Halvar picked up first one, then the other.

"Best made," he stated. "Girard had only the finest, didn't stint on important things like navigation."

Below the sextant and the spyglass was an open shelf that held what looked like ledgers; another shelf had rolled-up papers. Halvar unrolled the nearest one. Firebrand peered over his shoulder.

"Picture?" the Mahak asked, pointing to the lines and squiggles. "What's this for?"

"A map," Halvar explained. "Looks like he's made a few corrections." He pointed to two places where the outline was marked in two different colors of ink.

"This is not Manatas," Firebrand observed.

"I'm no seaman, and I can't tell where it is, but I'm sure there's someone on Manatas who can," Halvar said, allowing the map to roll back into its original shape. "I'll have to send someone here to take charge of these charts."

He turned to the small chest tucked into a space under the shelves.

"Clothes," he stated after a quick survey of the contents. "He wasn't planning to stay long on Manatas. There's his braies, or whatever it is that Franchen wear under their breeches. And a spare coat."

"No money chest? I thought the woman said he had money." Firebrand poked around in the sea chest.

"Kept it by him, in that pouch," Halvar decided. "Or perhaps, in his ditty-bag, the one he'd take ashore with him."

Firebrand poked at the rolls of maps and frowned at the books.

"The Franchen could read."

"No doubt," Halvar said, picking up one of the books and riffling the pages. "But this isn't a print book. It's written by hand. I think this is his logbook. All captains must keep a record, a log, of where they go, what they see, what the weather is, how far they go in a day."

"Why?" Firebrand was genuinely puzzled. "What difference does it make once the ship gets where it is bound?"

Halvar thought it over.

"I suppose, to let the next man on the same route know what to expect when he makes the trip."

"And if he cannot read or write?"

"Then he has someone do it who can." Halvar squinted at the cramped script. "This isn't Arabi. Maybe Franchen? I think we'll bring this to Selim, and see what the lad makes of it." He tucked the book safely under his coat, hoping the heavy material would shield it from the spray on their return trip.

He scanned the cabin again.

"We'll send one of his men over to collect his gear to send home to his family. And to take charge of these charts and maps. They could be useful to the calif when he comes back from his tour of inspection."

Firebrand had already left and was trying the other doors in the small area under the wooden ladder.

"More cabins," the Mahak declared.

"For passengers." Halvar stepped into the nearest one, and was overwhelmed by the sour odor of vomit mixed with the musk of expensive perfume. "I think this is where Milady Summersby spent the voyage with her maid," he decided. "According to Michel, she was sick for most of the time."

"What is this?" Firebrand held up a long piece of stiffened linen, with bones sewn into it and ribbons dangling from either end.

"I think that's what the Franchen women use to keep their bodices stiff and push their fronts up," Halvar said. "Not that I've seen one up close," he added hastily. "But this is all woman's gear, so this must be Milady Summersby's cabin for sure."

He scanned the debris, trying to make sense of the garments strewn about the tiny space.

"Skirts, skirts and more skirts."

Firebrand picked up what looked like a shirt made of fine linen.

"Very good cloth." He sniffed at it, and wrinkled his nose. "More smells."

"They say Franchen women use scent instead of soap," Halvar said. "And if Milady Summersby did use this cabin, I'd say they're right."

"No writing here," Firebrand commented as he tossed garments onto the bunkbed.

"Only one bed?" Halvar muttered, as they left the cabin and went back to the tiny space by the ladder.

"What about the other cabin?" Firebrand opened the other door.

Here things were much neater.

"Milord's man is better at keeping house than Milady's maid," Halvar observed. "And some of his gear is here, but I don't see his hat or coat. Nor his sword. All the Bretain milords carry them, whether they can use them or not, just to show who they are."

"And how many Bretain milords have you met?"

"One or two." Halvar shrugged. "Younger sons of Bretain milords, who had no inheritance coming to them. They came to Corduva to attend classes at the madrassa, as part of their education. When I was following Don Felipe, they would try to get close to him, to add to their consequence once they got back in Bretain.

"That way, they could say that they were friends with the ruler-to-be of Al-Andalus when they took their places at one of the petty courts in Bretain, maybe even at the High King's court. They spoke Erse and Franchen, and some tried to learn Arabi, but most of them stayed with the rest of the Bretains at the madrassa."

Firebrand sniffed contemptuously.

"Those Bretains! They make no provision for their own families."

"The younger sons have their own way to make, but they get by," Halvar said. "In the Dane-March, the oldest son gets the land, the second goes to sea, and whoever else is around becomes a frater. Or joins a free company."

"Like you."

"Like me."

There was more to it than that, but he had more important things to do than recite his life history.

They climbed back onto the upper deck. Firebrand frowned.

"No more singing," he said. "Look, another cabin."

He pointed to an open hatch midway between the bow and and stern. Together, Halvar and Firebrand approached it. No one appeared, although they could hear sounds coming from below.

Cautiously, Halvar edged down the ladder. They emerged into a long, low room, wider than the narrow deck above. Halvar had to walk carefully to avoid the beams of the deck overhead, which nearly touched the top of his fur hat.

"And now you know why they call these round ships," Halvar said. "They're built with a belly, to hold more cargo."

"But what kind of cargo is this?" Firebrand prowled around the space. "No boxes, no barrels." He poked at a small pile of something against the wall of the cabin. "Dung?"

"Passengers," Halvar said. "The mate, Michel, told me that on the voyage from Franchenland they carried women. They must have all stayed here, in this one room, all except the matron.

"Then, on the voyage from Kibbick to Manatas, the servants would stay here while Milord and Milady Summersby kept the cabins for themselves."

"No one else?" Firebrand prowled around the otherwise empty space. "Only the five?"

"Doesn't make much sense," Halvar agreed. "This ship's riding high. No cargo, only the five passengers. What can Girard have been thinking?"

Firebrand stopped his search to point to a row of iron rings riveted to the bulkhead.

"What about these? For animals?"

Halvar's frown deepened as he stared at the rings.

"Not animals, but treated like such. He'd been to Afrika. He was in Savana Port. He had a cargo of passengers, but not willing ones."

"He never used chains on the Franchen women!"

"Not them," Halvar said. "Others. We'd better get back to Manatas while we still can. That storm is taking its time, but it will get here before long, and I don't want to be stuck on this ship when it hits Manatas."

He emerged from the hatch to find a squad of large men doing the same from the forward hatch.

"*Avaunt!*"" The leader yelled.

And then the fight began.

Chapter 8

THE LEADER OF THE GROUP, A BURLY MAN IN
the woolen overshirt and knitted cap worn by Franchen sailors, barreled forward, waving a long club
with a spike on the end. Halvar had no time to identify the object. He was too busy evading it!

His task was made more difficult by the shifting
of the deck beneath his feet. The round ship was more
stable than a dhow, but between the sudden movement on board and the incoming tide, the ship began
to sway on its anchor-chain.

Three more men followed their leader across the
deck, all yelling loudly in Franchen. Halvar tried to explain, but they were in no mood for a discussion.

The leader slashed out with his marlinspike. Once
again Halvar was glad he had worn his old leather-lined cap under the araghoun fur hat. He ducked and
received a glancing blow, dodged another.

"I'm from Manatas," he gasped in Erse, hoping the sailor might have picked up some of that language in his travels. "I called out. Didn't you hear me?"

"*Sales sauvages!*"

The sailor either didn't speak Erse or wasn't going to listen. He tried another blow, and once again, the ship's movement thwarted his intentions.

Halvar grabbed at the woolen sweater, trying to stop the man's mad attack.

"Listen to me, you drunken ox!" he yelled in Danic, reverting to his native language.

The sailor threw the marlinspike away and lunged forward, trying to wrestle Halvar to the rail around the deck. If he couldn't smash this intruder, he'd throw him overboard!

Halvar was gripped by arms used to dealing with heavy canvas and heavier loads. Fingers like sausages throttled him as they staggered back and forth on the shifting deck. He could smell the reek of alcohol as the sailor tried to bite his ear.

He struggled to break free. One hand managed to get his dagger out of its sheath. He slid it upwards to slice the sailor's arm and break his grip.

The ship lurched again. The sailor yelled in pain and surprise, as Halvar shook him off.

"I'm not here to rob the ship!" Halvar shouted, trying to get through the fog of alcohol and suspicion.

It did no good. Once again the sailor tried to attack. This time Halvar had his knife ready, hoping to fend off this berserker.

Behind him, he heard a whoop. His attacker turned, just as the ship gave another lurch. Halvar felt his knife go into the man's chest as he fell forward.

He backed away to avoid the spurting blood. An arrow stuck out of his opponent's back. He pushed the cap out of his eyes. The two Locals he had thought

61

were waiting in the canoe had made their way up the ship's anchor to protect their leader.

The Mahak smashed one of the other sailors over the head with a war-club, while the Algonkin used a tomahawk on the third. Firebrand finished the job, slashing the fourth man across the throat with his knife, jumping out of the way of the blood.

Halvar swallowed hard to keep the bile from rising in his throat. He stared at the gory scene, then at his rescuers.

"What did you do that for?" he gasped.

"They were enemies. They were fighting." Muskrat said in halting Arabi.

"I wanted them alive!" Halvar said. "They're no use to anyone dead!"

"They would kill you." Seuleman pointed out. "Ilha will forgive me. I sought to save your life."

Halvar wiped his mouth.

"What Ilha does doesn't concern me, but I wanted them alive. Firebrand, go below and see if there's anyone else on board, and whatever you do, don't kill them!" He clung to the ship's rail, panting.

Firebrand said something in Munsi to his watchmen, who drew away from the dead sailors, muttering what Halvar assumed were formulas to keep the sailor's ghosts from haunting them. Some minutes later, the Mahak emerged from the hatch gripping the shirt of a shivering lad.

The boy took one look at Halvar and shrieked in fright. Then he saw the bodies and was noisily sick.

Firebrand dropped him to the deck.

"I found him hiding under a table. What is a child doing on a ship?

"Ship's boy," Halvar said. "Servant, sailor in training. Lad, d'ye speak Erse?"

The boy blinked at him.

"*Je ne comprends pas,*" he said, backing away in terror.

"And I don't have much Franchen," Halvar sighed. He tried again. "Girard...*mort.*" He made the universal sign of death, a finger across the throat.

At this news, the boy began to blubber.

"Why not kill him and finish the lot?" Firebrand asked in disgust.

"There's been enough killing," Halvar decreed. "Can we fit one more into that canoe of yours?"

The three Locals consulted in Munsi. Then Firebrand said, "He's not that big. But it will be a tight fit. And he must not move, or we will overturn."

Halvar turned to the boy and pointed to the rope ladder.

"Down there, laddie."

The boy took one look and shook his head violently.

Muskrat and Seulemon had gone down the anchor chain, taking the same route that had brought them aboard. They paddled the canoe back to the ladder, managing to keep it close to the ship's hull in spite of the surging tide.

Halvar gripped the rope with even more tenacity than he had when he climbed up, and hoped that the canoe would hold the extra weight of a small boy. He felt for the struts of the frail boat with one foot and eased himself down carefully. The boy stared down at him, then up at Firebrand.

"No choice, laddie. It's us or the deep." Halvar called up to him in Erse.

Firebrand propelled the youngster down the ladder, where Halvar grabbed him just in time to prevent him from falling into the waves. Firebrand slid down the ladder into the canoe and pushed them away from the round ship towards the island.

The trip back to Manatas Island was more terrifying than the trip out. The canoe was buffeted by waves that threatened to capsize the small craft. Muskrat and Seulemon paddled as strongly as they could but seemed to make little headway.

"Here!" Firebrand thrust a paddle at Halvar.

"Eh!" Halvar took it, "I don't know how to use this thing!"

"Dip and swing!" Firebrand demonstrated. "Unless you want to spend the rest of your days on one of those islands in the bay! So…Hay-ya! Hoy-ya!" He started a rhythmic chant. "Down when I go down, up when I go up."

"Hay-ya! Hoy-ya!" The Locals echoed, demonstrating the technique of paddling a canoe.

Halvar had rowed boats in Koben Haven harbor, but he'd never used anything like this. Still, he didn't want to end his days at the bottom of Manatas Bay, either.

"Like so!" Muskrat plied his paddle. "Hay-ya! Hoy-ya!"

Halvar squatted behind Muskrat, while Firebrand added his strength of arm to Seulemon.

"Keep the beat, boy. Hay-ya! Hoy-ya!"

The lad took up the chant. The canoe surged forward with each stroke of the paddles, bounding along with the current towards the island.

"Hay-ya! Hoy-ya!"

Each sweep of the paddle brought them closer to land.

Halvar was drenched in sweat, salt and spray by the time they reached the East Channel and the welcoming hands that pulled them onto the docks. Donal had commandeered a squad of mixed guardsmen and Locals to grab the ropes and haul the canoe up.

"What took you so long, Capitán?" Donal looked him over. "You've been in a fight! And who's this lad?"

"He's the ship's boy, all that's left of the crew of *Belle Fleur*," Halvar explained. "Best get him somewhere warm. He's had a shock. And then, I suppose, it's time for me to tackle Milord and Milady."

"Looking like that?" Donal was aghast. "Bad enough that servant of theirs wouldn't as much as open the door when I came to call on them. One look at you, and they'll laugh in your face."

Halvar looked down at his coat, once so fine, now spattered with blood, grime, salt and tar.

"You're right, I can't talk to a Bretain milord like this. It would reflect badly on Don Felipe and the sultan." He turned to Firebrand, but the Mahak and his two watchmen were back on the water in their canoe. "Hoy! Stay here! There's more to be done!" he called after them.

"They're going back to the Mahak village," Donal surmised, "Probably doing something with their shaman to keep away Franchen ghosts."

"Nothing for it, Tenente, you'll have to come with me. Do you know any Franchen?"

"A bit," Donal admitted.

"Good. Tell this lad we're taking him to safety, that he won't get hurt, and if anyone asks what happened on board *Belle Fleur*, he's to tell the truth, which is that he saw nothing because he was hiding under a table in the crew's mess."

With that, Halvar trudged across the plaza to the warmth of the Mermaid Taberna.

Chapter 9

THE WAILING CALL OF THE MUEZZIN FROM the waterfront muskat vied with the Roumi Rite chapel bells in reminding the the people of Manatas it was time for afternoon prayers. While the vendors and buyers of fish and vegetables prostrated themselves to call on Ilha and his Prophet, Donal obediently went down on one knee to recite the Patri Nostri.

Halvar remained standing but gripped his amulet and thanked the Redeemer, Mother Mara and Thor for their help in his latest escape from death. He assured them that he had not meant to kill the sailor having had no choice in the matter—it was the sailor's life or his.

And he was not responsible for anything the Mahak or Algonkin had done on his behalf. He could only hope the coming Yule would make their judgment more lenient when it came time to assess his eventual fate in the next life.

The cabin boy gazed about him in bewilderment.

"Kristo?" Donal asked.

The boy nodded, obviously relieved to find some point of contact with the strangers who had taken him from the ship. Then, Donal yanked him down to recite the proper rubric, and they both finished by making the sign of the crux.

Religious duties done, Halvar shoved the boy ahead of him until they reached the doors of the taberna.

"This lad's the only one left of those on board the *Belle Fleur*," he commented. "Those Locals are like bear-shirts when their blood is up. I can see why no one wants to get on their wrong side."

"The Algonkin aren't so bad, but the Mahak are fierce, and the Huron are worse," Donal assured him. "They don't have pretty rules when it comes to warfare, like they do in Oropa. Their aim is to kill as many of the enemy as they can. If they take a prisoner, it's to have sport with him later. Ask Fru Glick, she saw what they did to her man."

"She told me some," Halvar said. There was probably more, but he didn't want to know all the gory details.

Hannes Zilberstam bustled up to them, tut-tutting at the state of Halvar's new coat.

"I know, I know," Halvar told him. "It's done for."

"Maybe not," Hannes said, turning him about to examine the garment. "If these bloodstains are fresh, maybe Fru Marta can get them out. Woman, come out of the kitchen!"

The Danic cook trotted out, ladle in hand.

"What d'ye want, old man? I've got a stew bubbling, the bread's baking, what else d'ye need?"

"Capitan Danske's coat. Can you clean it?"

"What've you been doing, butchering hogs?" Marta frowned at the stains of tar, salt water, and blood that marred the green wool.

"Not my blood, and I didn't mean to kill him," Halvar protested as Hannes and Marta divested him of his garment. "What about this coat? Can you clean it? It's only just out of Yussuf the Tailor's shop. I'd hate to throw it away so soon."

"Cold water, lye soap—I can get this clean," Margetta assured him.

"Put it on my bill," Halvar told Hannes.

He looked around the room, now filling with fishermen and their customers, and spotted two men at the backgammon tables, a pair he recognized as professional gamblers.

"Lukas, Baltasar!" He beckoned them over.

The taller of the two, a dark-skinned man of Halvar's age wearing the kaftan and turban favored by Andalusian merchants, salaamed respectfully.

"*Salaam aleikum*, Don Alvaro," Baltasar greeted him. "What can I do for you today? It's early for a game."

"Not tables, but talk. Can either of you speak Franchen?"

The shorter man, a slightly-built youth in an embroidered shirt worn over baggy trousers of the sort favored by madrassa students, said, "I know some Franchen, Don Alvaro."

"Good. Tell this lad we mean him no harm, that we're not pirates or thieves but the Town Guard. And tell him that his captain, Franz Girard, is dead. Find out all you can about that ship and its crew. And especially about the passengers."

Baltasar's eyes widened at the news. Lukas spoke to the boy in Franchen, looking sorrowful. The boy gasped and spoke at length to the two gamblers, pointing to the ship in the harbor.

Lukas questioned him in a sharper tone. The boy answered, at first hesitantly then with more assurance. When he was finished, he wiped his eyes with a sodden sleeve and sniffled mournfully.

Lukas reported, "His name is Jeannot, he's the ship's boy, which means he does whatever they tell him to do. He came on board at Kibbick. His father's a Franchen fisherman, his mother's dead.

"He didn't know they were coming to Manatas. No one did. It was an odd decision, but it was up to the captain to set the course, not for anyone else to question it.

"When they got through the gap between the islands and into the bay, the captain left him and the other four to guard the ship and the rest of the crew went ashore. The captain promised Jeannot and the other four could go and ashore as soon as the others had had their fill of women and shore food and drink.

"Michel Primero was supposed to return in the morning, but the lad thinks Primero got drunk and forgot about them."

The boy added something, with a loud sniff more of disgust than sorrow.

"The other four got tired of waiting for their drink and tapped the rhum kegs," Lukas translated. "They weren't supposed to—the rhum was in the cargo bay, meant for buyers in Terra Mara."

"I *thought* they were drunk," Halvar commented. "Ask the lad about the passengers. The milord and milady from Kibbick."

Jeannot grimaced. "Milord…Milady," he spat out.

"I don't think he liked them," Lukas said with a smirk.

There was more conversation in Franchen. Marta appeared from the kitchen with a steaming bowl of hot soup and a woolen shirt.

"Get that wet thing off the child before he catches his death!" she ordered. "Here, boy, put this on."

Before he could object, she yanked his thin linen shirt over his head, revealing a back marred with bruises.

Lukas's smirk turned into a snarl.

"I don't doubt this lad has had bad treatment," he said. "And if I know sailors, there's worse. But you're safe with us, Jeannot," he told the boy, switching from Arabi to Franchen as Baltasar eased the clean shirt over the boy's shoulders.

They led him to their table, where he applied himself to the soup while the adults talked over his head in Arabi.

"As far as he knows, the passengers were taken on in Kibbick. They brought several trunks with clothes, and some crates with other gear, but he doesn't know anything else about them. He had to serve the servants and didn't like them. The old woman was sick for most of the voyage, the mistress kept to her cabin to attend her. But once or twice Milady came on deck, and when she did, the captain was always very attentive."

"What about Milord?" Halvar shivered in his damp linen shirt.

"Milord was on deck every day, getting in the way, according to Jeannot. He and the bodyguard would fence with swords, or sit on the deck and drink some of the stuff they'd brought with them from Kibbick. And the manservant was always hanging over Primero's shoulder, and watching every day when the captain took his measurements and wrote in his book.

70

"Captain Girard told them not to get in the way of the sailors, but Milord told him that since he was paying for the trip, he would do as he liked. And that his man, Edgar, he was in Milord's pay, and Milord wished him to learn everything he could about navigation, in case the captain met with an accident."

Halvar tugged at his mustache.

"And what did Captain Girard think of that idea?"

Jeannot spoke up again. Lukas translated.

"'Dunno. I just heard them quarreling, but then I was told to get to the galley, to help Cookie. So, I don't know if this Edgar learned navigation or no. I'm supposed to, but it's all numbers, and I don't like numbers, so I'm mostly in the galley or up aloft, working the sails.'"

Hannes had sent one of his servers upstairs to fetch Halvar's spare coat. Now the halfling appeared with the garment, a serviceable Town Guard coat modified to fit Halvar's greater breadth across the shoulders by the addition of gussets at the shoulder seams.

He shrugged into the coat, adjusted his leather-lined cap and araghoun fur hat, and and fastened his belt, with his trusty dagger that had saved his life once again safely in its sheath.

"Tenente Donal, did you get anything out of the servants at all?" He brushed a finger over his mustache again to make sure it, too, was neat.

Donal sputtered indignantly.

"That high-and-mighty valet, or whatever he calls himself, said that Milord was a Bretain, and not accountable to Andalusians. And I got an earful of abuse from the maid. What a mouth she's got!"

"This is not Bretain, and Milord Summersby will do well to remember where he is." Halvar turned to leave. "Come along, Tenente! We'll show these Bretains the Manatas Town Guard is not some village watch!"

He strode forth, nearly bumping into Tenente Flores and Selim at the door.

"Have you found Ibo?" Halvar demanded.

"That's what I came to tell you," Flores panted. "His donkey-cart came in, but not him. The Emir is furious. He's got his people out looking for Ibo. If something's happened to the poor fellow…" His voice trailed off. "Why? What do you want with him?"

"He saw or heard the murderer," Halvar stated flatly. "And whatever Girard may have done to provoke someone to kill him, Ibo was an innocent bystander. If he's been killed, I won't have it!

"Tenente, you and your men keep up the search. I want that man found! And while you're at it, Girard sent a message, we don't know what, to someone, we don't know who. Probably by one of those lads that haunt the waterfront looking for someone to send them somewhere. Find him, too. But most of all, find Ibo!"
Halvar turned to Donal.

"You come with me, Tenente Donal. Just in case these two Bretains speak some kind of Erse I don't know. Selim, what are you doing here? I thought I told you to find out what you could about the ship and its crew. Don't tell me the tallyman was ready with the answer so fast."

"Yes, in fact, he was," Selim said triumphantly. "Kemal the Tallyman was very forthcoming when he heard there was a ship in the harbor that hadn't paid its docking toll. He checked the records for me immediately.

"You were right. Captain Girard was last here in spring with people from Savana Port—that Afrikan merchant with the Cherokee wife, the one who was poisoned at the Fall Feria. Neither Girard or his ship has been back since. As for Kemal, he didn't expect any more round ships until spring, so he'd shut down the tally-booth. He's not pleased Girard didn't announce himself as soon as he got ashore. A ship as large as that is good for a considerable sum for the calif's treasury."

"Interesting," Halvar mused. "Baltasar, Lukas, take this lad to his shipmates at Maison Rouge, if you please."

There was a squawk of protest from Jeannot.

"I don't think that would be a good idea," Lukas said, after a whispered conversation with Baltasar. "Better for him to stay with us for a bit. We've got lodgings up the hill, at Mama Sharon's mokka-house. He'll be safer there."

Halvar tugged at his mustache, weighing one possibility against another. If the boy had been abused on the ship, perhaps he'd be better off with the two gamblers and their lady friends.

"All right," he decided. "And let me know if he tells you anything more about Girard or Milord and Milady Summersby. There's something nasty going on, and this lad may be in danger."

He regarded Selim and Donal, then sighed.

"Selim, Donal, you're with me. Flores, keep looking for that Afrikan, and find that messenger who was hanging around Maison Rouge last night. I'll take two of your people with me. We have to remind these Bretains they're in Andalusian territory now."

He strode out into the waning sunlight to face that most formidable of enemies—a Bretain milord.

Chapter 10

THE BRICK HOUSE PREVIOUSLY INHABITED
by Jacques and Lizette Tavernier was the middle one
of three, each on its own small plot of land, on the
lane known as Pearl Street, because it had been paved
with oyster shells. Unlike the large blocks of villas
farther north, these were built in the Oropan style, with
peaked roofs and small leaded-glass windows looking out onto the walls of the Rabat.

Each house was surrounded by trees whose last
few leaves fluttered down in the rising wind. Across
the lane from the houses was a fenced-in yard containing a shed where a flock of bedraggled hens clucked
and scratched for whatever bits they could find, while
their rooster strutted among them, loudly proclaim-
ing his territory.

Outside the fence, a gaggle of geese pecked at the
ground between the shells, picking up bits of grass
and honking loudly at anyone who dared to stop them.

The ever-present gulls wheeled and swooped over the yard, looking for anything the other birds may have missed.

A bare patch of earth still held the remnants of what had been a vegetable plot with stems and stalks of cabbages, escouash, maiz and beans littering the ground, food for geese and small singing birds on their way south. It was a tiny bit of Oropa tucked into the space between the Rabat and the square buildings that lined the Broad Way.

There were no men in sight, but a stout woman in the solid-colored wool skirt and bodice favored by Danic women was sweeping dried leaves from the path that led from the house on the right to the street. The doorway of the house on the left was filled with a woman in a tartan skirt and shawl who clutched a bawling baby while she bargained with a Local woman for the vegetables in a basket. A teenaged girl, also in Danic dress, slouched past the armed men, swinging a bucket as she led a goat, apparently ready for milking, towards the shed.

All the women stopped what they were doing to stare at Halvar and his party as they marched to the one door that was shut tight against the rest of Manatas. Halvar led the way, followed by Donal and Selim. Flores's two guardsmen brought up the rear of the parade, their halberds over their shoulders. They ignored the gazes of the curious women.

Halvar straightened his fur hat and squared his shoulders.

There is no reason to be awed by these Bretains, he told himself. He was the Calif's Hireling, a personal representative of Don Felipe, the nominal ruler of Al-Andalus-In-Exile, and the equal of anyone in Al-Andalus. He was a freeborn Dane, whose father farmed a good portion under the protection of the Thane, who answered to the High King in Koben Haven, which made him as good as anyone in the Dane-March. He need bow to no one except out of politeness, least of all this Milord Summersby. He would not be intimidated by that overbearing air of superiority that every Bretain milord he had ever encountered seemed to carry about him, as if the people of his tiny island chain were destined to rule the world.

He reminded himself of this as he banged on the door.

"Manatas Town Guard! Open!" he called out, first in Arabi, then in Erse.

The door opened a crack. He could see a man in the tight breeches and dark, fitted coat fancied by the Franchen.

"Who dares to call on Milord Summersby?" the man demanded in Erse.

Halvar tugged at his mustache. The man sounded like a cultured scholar, not a rough servant.

Conversation proceeded in Erse.

"I am Capitán Halvar Danske with news for Milord. Let me in, if you please."

"And if I don't please?" The man sounded vaguely amused.

"Then we come in anyway," Donal retorted. "I told you I'd be back with the capitán, and here he is. We want to see your master, you fool. Open up!"

"Milord Summersby is not at home."

"Bollocks!" Donal snapped. "Where would he go? He's not a merchant, nor is he a student or professor at the madrassa. He hasn't presented himself to our excellent sultan, either. So, he's got to be here." He finished with a decided nod, as if to say, *That is as demonstrated!*

Halvar took over the conversation again.

"We are here to inform Milord Summersby of the sad death of his friend, Captain Franz Girard."

The neighbor women sidled closer, eager to hear more. This was grand news, food for gossip at the souk! Halvar used their clear curiosity to press his case.

"Do you want to draw the attention of every Oropan in Manatas to this house?"

The door opened to reveal a man of Halvar's age, slender and dark, his hair neatly tied back with a ribbon, dressed as observed in the dark coat and knee-breeches worn by respectable Franchen merchants. His head was bare, unlike most of the Islim and Yehudit, who usually wore some kind of hat or cap, indoors and out. He was neatly shaved.

"What do you mean, coming in force in this rude manner?"

"I sent one of my men to ask Milord Summersby some questions. He told me you refuse to acknowledge the authority of the Town Guard. I am here to remind you and your master that you are under the rule of Al-Andalus. A murder has been committed, and you and your master are requested to assist us in finding the killer."

"A murder? Of whom? And what has it to do with us?"

"The body of Franz Girard has been found," Halvar repeated, glaring at the servant.

The women from the two cottages gasped and chattered in the Manatas patois that combined Arabi, Erse and Munsi, all laced with allusions that baffled anyone not from Manatas.

"We have been told it was Girard who brought Milord Summersby to Manatas. Perhaps he can tell us who would want to do the captain harm."

"I see." He nodded, thinking it over. "Under those circumstance, you may enter. I will inform Milord of your arrival."

He allowed Halvar to brush past him into the one large room that comprised most of the cottage. Donal and Selim hastened in after him, leaving the two guards to stand outside the door.

The interior of the house hadn't changed since Halvar had been there two months before. The main room was filled with bulky furniture—a heavily carved long table and two wooden armchairs with solid, carved backs took up most of the space in the center of the room. A set of shelves had been attached to one wall, with a closed cabinet below.

The fireplace was across from the door, its chimney shared with the kitchen on the other side of the wall. A door opened into the kitchen, the only other room on that story. A narrow staircase let upward to the second floor, where Halvar assumed there would be sleeping quarters.

He again noted the gruesome artwork that filled cottage. One painted panel over the fireplace depicted the Redeemer on his crux, writhing in torment. Paintings on either side of the windows showed holy men of olden times being tortured for their refusal to deny their faith. All were in bright colors, with plenty of blood spurting from wounds in tortured bodies. No wonder Hannes Zilberstam preferred to sleep on a pallet under the stairs in the comfortable fug of the Mermaid Taberna!

His attention was drawn away from the ghastly art by a peevish voice The man descending the stairs was fair-haired and blue-eyed, as Halvar was, but shorter and heavier, dressed in the nipped-in coat and tight breeches of a Franchen aristocrat.

"Edgar, who are these people? What is this about Girard?" he asked in Erse, drawling his vowels and clipping his consonants in a way that made Donal draw a sudden breath.

"Milord…" the servant began, but Halvar broke in.

"I am Capitán Don Alvaro Danico of the Manatas Town Guard, and Captain Franz Girard is dead," he said bluntly.

"How?" Milord blinked in astonishment. "He was well enough when we parted."

"He was killed sometime early this morning. I sent one of my men to inform you, but he was refused entrance by this servant of yours."

"Oh, Edgar is very protective," Milord said with a wave of his hand. "But this is appalling, truly appalling! Girard dead? How? By whose hand?"

"I cannot say at this time," Halvar said. "The body is being examined by our doctor."

Selim had found a place to sit on a long chest under one of the windows. Donal remained by the door.

Milord sat down heavily on one of the two chairs.

"This is dreadful!" he sputtered. "Girard told me we would only put in here for a day or two, until the storm passed. Then we could resume our journey to Bel-Mar'"

"That's what we Bretains call Bella Mara, Sultan Calvera's new town," Donal explained. "Takes too long for these high-up Bretains to say all those extra words."

Halvar took the other chair without waiting for an offer.

"So, Milord, if you didn't expect to come to Manatas, what are you doing here? What do you know of Captain Girard's business interests in Manatas?"

"That is no concern of yours, Capitán, or whatever you call yourself." Milord sniffed. "And I had no interest in any of Girard's other affairs. I paid him to take me to Terra Mara. If he had any other business in mind, he did not confide in me."

Halvar regarded the Bretain impassively.

"It *is* my concern, because the man who carried you here has been killed, and no one knows why, and it is my job to see that all visitors to Manatas are safe from such violence. As far as I know, the only ones who had anything to do with him here, from the time he arrived until his death, are the people from his ship, which means his crew and you and your lady and your servants. So, Milord, I must ask you to give me your movements from the time you arrived here until now."

"This is impertinence!" Summersby exploded. "How dare you question me? Do you know who I am?"

"No, I do not," Halvar said. "Tell me, Milord, who are you? And why are you sailing in waters controlled by Al-Andalus?"

"Al-Andalus? Hispania, you mean!" Summersby sneered. "And if you must know, I have a legacy, some land in Terra Mara. It was willed to me by a Franchen relation who settled there under the amnesty given by Calif Don Carlus when he appointed a Kristo to be sultan there." He sounded as if he had learned this by heart. His voice changed as he went on, sounding more aggrieved than confident. "I was supposed to go to West Caster, but the ship wound up in Kibbick. So, I had to hire another ship to take me south, which ship was *Belle Fleur* under Captain Girard."

"I see," Halvar said when Summersby stopped for breath.

Milord passed his tongue over his lips.

"Edgar, is there anything in this place fit to eat or drink?"

"I believe there is some wine, but whether it is any good is problematic. Sieur Devallon has gone to the marketplace they call a souk to find some more servants and some foodstuffs."

Edgar produced a bottle and a glass and poured a small sample for his master's assessment. Summersby sniffed at the liquid, took a taste, and made a face.

"Faugh! This is dreadful! What sort of people drink this stuff? I thought this house had been owned by the tavernkeepers!"

"Alcohol is forbidden in Manatas, according to sharia law," Halvar reminded him. "Mullah Abadul is very strict about it; you might want to develop a taste for mokka. There's also a root drink, and plenty of cider."

"Or you can send for ale from the Gardens of Paradise," Donal put in with a sardonic smile.

Summersby grimaced.

"Ale? Cider? What sort of place is this? I was told that Manatas was civilized. How can a place without wine be called civilized?"

"Manatas has been in Andalusian hands for fifty years," Halvar reminded him. "If you intend to stay here, Milord, you'll have to get used to Andalusian ways."

"I don't intend to stay here," Summersby protested. "I never wanted to come here. That was Girard's idea."

"Ah, yes—Captain Girard. What can you tell me of Captain Girard?"

Summersby took another sip of his wine and, by his expression, decided it was even worse than he'd thought.

"I can't tell you much. I met him in Kibbick, as I said. The captain who brought me to Nova Mundum was not willing to continue south, and I had no desire to spend a winter in Kibbick. The only company other than soldiers were merchants and locals. I had been told that there were proper gentry in Kibbick, but that was not true.

"At least, in Bel-Mar I expect to find someone with whom I can converse. All they talk about in Kibbick is trade or the war with the Locals." He regarded his glass gloomily. "I don't know what I shall do in Manatas. From what I've seen so far, it's full of Andalusian merchants. And craftsmen. No one for a gentleman to consort with."

"There's a sizable group of Bretains in Green Village," Halvar offered, with a glance at Donal, whose red face looked as if he were ready to explode at any moment.

"Mechanicals, farmers, fishermen!" Summersby said with a sneer.

Selim spoke up from her perch on the chest.

"I suppose you can go hunting, if you find a Local guide. Leon said that Bretain milords like to hunt."

Summersby's face lightened.

"Hunting? What kind of game is there?"

"Deer," Donal answered. "Plenty of those about, especially at this time of year, when they come down from the mountains, and the bucks go into rut. And wolves, if you're interested in something more dangerous."

Halvar wondered whether he should warn Summersby about some of the smaller creatures in Manatas, then decided this pompous popinjay deserved what he would get if he disturbed a sekonk in its wanderings.

He got back to the main reason for his visit.

"Do not take offense, Milord, but I must ask, where were you last night and this morning?"

Summersby turned to his manservant.

"Where did we go yesterday, Edgar?"

Edgar said smoothly, "We cast anchor in the bay just before sunset, when the bells in the chapel were ringing for evening prayers and the callers in the muskats were doing the same. Captain Girard had assured us that we would be made welcome at the Mermaid Taberna, where there was a Franchen landlord and his wife in charge, and that they would give us lodging and food for as long as it took the storm to blow itself out. But when we arrived at the taberna, the Franchen was not there."

"There have been a few changes since last spring," Donal said with a satisfied smirk.

"So we discovered. Instead of a Franchen, we were greeted by a Danic seaman, who knew nothing of Captain Girard and would not let us into his upper floor."

"I should hope not!" Halvar muttered.

"Then he brought us to this house, which had been untenanted for two months. It was very nearly uninhabitable! Mice had made homes in the beds, there was no fire in the stove, the kitchen was filthy. There were no furnishings except for the bedsteads upstairs and the table and chairs here in this front room. It is not a suitable place for Milord Summersby!"

"But it's what there was, so we took it," Summersby said with a heavy sigh. "And Edgar and Dame Brigitte spent all night making it fit to live in."

"Indeed, we did!"

A tall, thin woman in a dark skirt and jacket worn under a white apron, her hair tucked into a lace-trimmed gathered cap, marched down the stairs, followed by a vision in pale green silk. The younger fair hair artfully curled, her round face carefully painted with cosmetics that emphasized her blue eyes and pink lips. Milady Summersby and her maid had come to add their comments to the discussion.

There was a gasp from Donal and a muffled squawk from Selim. Halvar took in the elaborate hairstyle, the fine garments, and the sparkling jewels dangling from her ears and around her neck as Milady swept around the room to stand beside her husband and decided this was going to be more difficult than he thought. Clearly, Milady Summersby was no meek Andalusan wife, content to hide behind a veil in the harem.

"What is all this about Captain Girard being dead? He can't be dead, he's got to get us to Bel-Mar." Milady's voice was shrill, her Erse flavored with Franchen overtones.

"Alas, Milady," Halvar said. "He is, indeed, dead, and his ship is abandoned in the harbor."

"But there were men on board," Summersby sputtered.

"Not anymore," Halvar said with a rueful look at Donal. "They thought my Mahak watchmen were thieves. The Mahak fought back."

"Oh, no!" Milady gasped.

She gripped the back of Summersby's chair and seemed to stagger. The maid held her arm and guided her toward the chair Halvar occupied, grating out, "Get up, you lout! Can't you see Milady is ill?"

She glared at him, and he gallantly rose and allowed Milady to sink into the seat.

"There, you sit there." Dame Brigitte fussed over her mistress then turned her disdainful eyes on Halvar and Donal. "It is as Edgar said. We spent all last night getting this sty fit for a gentleman and a lady," she snarled. "And what folk we are among!"

"Goodly folk, Brigitte," Edgar tried to soothe her. "The Danic woman brought us a cheese and a loaf of bread, and some milk, fresh from the goat. A Bretain person has promised us one of his sausages."

Dame Brigitte would not be soothed.

"A cheesemonger and a sausage-maker! Fine folk for Milady Summersby to associate with! We are not used to such, I can tell you."

Halvar took in the maid's coarse features—the large nose, wide mouth, and shrewd eyes under shaggy eyebrows, coupled with her height and demeanor—and decided the respectable housewives on either side might do well to refuse to associate with her.

Edgar turned to Halvar.

"I suppose it would be good policy for Milord Summersby to present himself to the ruler here, who-ever he is," he said. "How long will it take to get to him, to whom should I offer a present, and how much will suffice?"

"Sultan Petrus will receive you whenever you show up at the Rabat. He's an old soldier, doesn't keep a court, and is always ready for news as to the state of affairs in Oropa. We haven't heard much since the ships left after the Fall Feria. Yours is the first that has put in, other than the fishing boats from West Cast-er.

"As for bribes, none needed. You're talking to the person who can present you to the sultan, and I don't take bribes."

"More fool you," Donal muttered, just loud enough for Halvar to hear.

"This sultan…is he married?" Milady asked sud-denly with a calculating glint in her eyes. "I've heard that Islim men marry several wives at a time."

"Oh, yes, Milady, that he is." Halvar grinned un-der his mustache. "He's got one wife in Al-Andalus, and another here in Manatas. Lady Ayesha."

"Then I shall present myself to her," Milady de-clared. "At least there's some sort of Society in this miserable place. Brigitte! Help me to change my dress. Oh, dear, most of my baggage is still on the ship. If we are to stay on this island for any length of time, my trunks must be brought to me."

Milady's sartorial distress was interrupted by the sounds of a scuffle outside.

'You can't go in!"

"Nonsense, man! I belong here!"

Donal opened the door to see what was going on.

A tall, dark man in a well-worn leather jacket and baggy breeches, much like the garb Halvar had worn when he first came to Manatas, strode into the room, followed by a stout woman in the dark dress and white cap of a Yehudit and a brawny Afrikan in a multicolored wool caftan, his head covered with a small knitted cap.

Halvar stared at the newcomers and tugged at his mustache. The Yehudit woman and the Afrikan man were strangers, but he recalled the Oropan vividly. The last time he had seen that face, it had been looming over him, twisted with rage, and he had just had the pounding of his young life. Those broad shoulders, the long legs, the dark beard, all remained vividly in his memory, as the only time he'd ever been beaten by anyone close to his own size.

"God be with ye, Devallon," he said. "Tell me, what's one of the imperator's Musket-men doing here in Mantas?"

Chapter 11

HALVAR THOUGHT HE'D SEEN THE LAST OF THAT mocking face many years ago. This was the one who had beaten him down into the muck of a town on the border between the Dane-march and Franchenland during what was supposed to be a friendly game of kick-the-bladder that had disintegrated into a brawl. Bile rose in his throat as he recalled the arrogance of the company of Franchen who had carried brand-new muskets.

How they had sneered at the Danes and their old-fashioned pikes and lances. How they had swaggered through the streets of that small town, where both companies had taken winter quarters after an agreement had been reached by their respective commanders.

There had been encounters, not all of them pleasant. Finally, the Franchen had challenged the Danes to the match, and the result had been mayhem. The Danes had won, but at a heavy cost. The Franchen had left the town well before the Danes, and the aftermath had been even worse than the brawl.

Old Sergeant Olaf had treated Halvar's bruises with ointment and soothed his wounded feelings with wise sayings. Halvar had accepted both but had privately sworn that if he ever met one of those musket-men again, there would be a reckoning.

The Oropan stared at Halvar.

"Do I know you?" he asked, his dark brows twisted into a frown.

"We met, once on a time," Halvar said evenly in Erse. "You are Devallon, of the Franchen Company of Musket-men. The last time I saw your company, it was just before the battle at Pisa. Your commanders chose to leave rather than face the cannons ranged against them. I don't know if you were among them."

"Oh, I was there, and they made the right decision, considering the Free Company of Danes remained to defend the city and got cut to pieces. We went to Hispania, joined the imperator's army, and got well paid for it," Devallon retorted.

His frown dissolved into a guffaw.

"By the Crux, it's the brave lad! What's your name? Halvar, that's it! The one who thought he'd defend the honor of the Danes and challenged me to a fight when we kicked the bladder in…what was that town again? No matter, it was a good while ago. I didn't recognize you with that bush under your nose! I see you've come up in the world. Capitán of Guards, is it? Well, well, things change, don't they."

Halvar smoothed the mustache in question.

"They do, indeed. So, I ask you again, Musket-man Devallon, what are you doing here in Manatas?"

"As you can see, I'm no longer a Musket-man, It's plain Sieur Devallon now. I'm serving Milord Henry

Summersby." He turned to milord. "I've found you a cook and a general serving-man," he stated, pointing to the Yehudit woman and Afrikan man standing behind him. "They can come in every day for five purple wum-pum each. That's a half a silver Bretain penny.

"Outrageous!" sputtered Milord. "I don't pay Edgar anything like that! I could get a servant in Bretain for a copper penny a day, and in Franchenland for less. I only pay *you* one dinar a month."

"But we're not in Bretain or Franchenland," Devallon reminded him. "And most of the folk in Manatas either already have servants, or do their own work."

"Isn't there a slave market?" Milord asked peevish-ly. "We're in Andalusian territory, they have slaves."

"Not in Manatas!" Donal stated, drawing Deval-lon's attention away from Milord. "Not in West Cast-er, and not in Manatas. I don't know about any other territory or sultanate, but we don't buy and sell per-sons here."

"Slaves we have," Selim put in from her post un-der the window. "But they come from the Afrikan ter-ritories, or from Al-Andalus."

"So, if you want servants, you must hire them." De-vallon pointed to the woman. "This is Rachel, she will come and cook the daily meals but insists on cleaning the kitchen to her own standards first. And she is con-versant with the regulations concerning both Islim and Yehudit cookery, so we will not incur the wrath of their formidable mullah. The man is Juba, he does the heavy lifting."

Milord's face grew redder.

"Islim? Yehudit? Afrikan? Is there no Oropan Kris-to who will serve us?"

"Not here in Manatas," Devallon said ruefully. "For that, you would have to go to Green Village, where most

89

of the Bretains have their own community. There is even an Erse Rite fratery and chapel."

"You've found out a good deal for someone who's just arrived," Halvar mused.

Devallon smirked. "I've got a little Arabi, and I'm not afraid to ask questions."

"What about answering them?" Halvar countered. "For instance, when did you last see Captain Girard? And what were you doing early this morning?"

"I last saw Captain Girard when we left the taberna, after he put us into the hands of the Danic landlord. What's this about?"

"Girard is dead," Milord told him. "According to this fellow, he was found this morning in an alley."

Devallon shook his head.

"That's ridiculous. Why kill Girard? Who did it?"

"The very questions I was going to ask you," Halvar said. "How did you come to know him? And why are you in the employ of this Bretain milord? I thought you'd be with the Musket-men forever."

"It's a long tale," Devallon began.

"Then it's best told at the Rabat," Halvar decided. "As I have told you, Milord Summersby, you and your fine lady should present yourselves to Sultan Petrus at the Rabat as soon as you can. It's the great fortress at the tip of the island. I'm sure Heer Devallon can find it for you."

"That soon?" Devallon looked at Halvar in amazement. "Are there no palms to grease, no officials to please?"

"Sultan Petrus is an old army man," Halvar assured him. "He runs Manatas like an army camp. No courtiers, and just the Town Guards, of which I am the head. If I say you see him, you do. And my palm is not to be greased."

Milord had other objections.

"And how am I supposed to get there? I have no horse on this miserable island. I don't see any chair-bearers. How do people get about in this benighted place?"

"We walk," Halvar said. "Or take a donkey cart. Heer Devallon can fetch one from the Broad Way for you. They charge one white wumpum per ride—don't be talked into anything more."

"Walk?" Milord echoed. "Donkey cart? These streets are filthy with dung from those donkeys. And there are geese everywhere! They were honking all night, Devallon. We cannot remain here, you must find us other lodgings!"

"I'll do what I can, Milord," Devallon said. "But perhaps you should do as Capitán Halvar suggests first and pay your respects to the sultan. He might be able to persuade some of the better sort of people to accommodate you and Milady while you are in Manatas."

Milord grumpily finished his glass of wine. Rachel and the Afrikan followed Edgar to the kitchen, from which emerged cries of disgust and imprecations in several languages.

Halvar beckoned to his own people and rallied his troops outside the house.

"Well, Tenente Donal? What do you think of this Milord Summersby?"

Donal shook his head. "He's Bretain, all right, but he's no milord. He don't speak right."

"What do you mean, speak right? He talks Erse, doesn't he?" Selim said.

"Erse, yes, but the wrong kind for a milord. They talk like the people at court. He sounds like one of the folk come from the north country, far from the gentry of Londinium. And he wasn't taught at Oxenbridge, either. That servant, though? He was, from the sound of him."

"And I don't like his wife," Selim put it. "She smells of bad perfume and has too much paint on her face. And that maid is just plain rude."

"We'll see what your father makes of them," Halvar said as he led his party back to the Rabat.

Chapter 12

THE SHORT WINTER DAY WAS COMING TO A close as they marched up to the gates of the Rabat, where Flores was waiting with Zoltan and Fergus.

"We've got the sailors from the *Belle Fleur*," Flores told him. "I've put them into the cells."

"What did you do that for?" Halvar asked.

"Soften them up a bit, if they see what's in store for them," Zoltan said with a malicious grin.

Halvar glared at his subordinates.

"I thought I made it clear I won't have torture used on witnesses. It does no good. I don't want to hear what they think I want. I want to hear the truth."

"The truth? Those Franchen were liars in their mothers' wombs." Flores spat on the flagstones of the courtyard. "Kristos—Roumi Rite, at that. You won't get anything out of them. It's clear to me, Capitán. One of them wanted their captain dead, they're all in it."

"I don't think so," Halvar said. "The crewmen on board the ship defended it to the death. *Their* deaths." He took a long, shuddering breath then said, "Release the sailors and bring them to Dr. Moise's dead-house. I want to make sure we've got Captain Girard there."

"What makes you think we don't?" Selim asked.

"We've been fooled before," Halvar said curtly.

Fergus and Zoltan trotted across the courtyard to the cells while Flores followed Halvar, Donal and Selim into the relative warmth of Dr. Moise's domain. The tall Afrikan was warming his hands over a brazier of hot charcoal. He wore a heavy wool tunic over a striped kutton caftan and a knitted cap pulled over his ears.

"What have you learned from the late Captain Girard?" Halvar asked.

"That, as I thought, he was stabbed," Dr. Moise said. "with a long slender object, triangular in shape."

He led Halvar and Selim into the examining room, where the late Captain Franz Girard had been placed on the table in the middle of the room. His clothing lay next to him, neatly folded. A small pile of oddments was set next to the clothing.

Donal and Flores hung back in the doorway, unwilling to be too close to the presence of Death. Selim's fascinated gaze was riveted on the body. She sketched furiously in her ever-present notebook.

"I didn't have to examine him further," Dr. Moise went on. "His cause of death is obvious. He was otherwise in good health, well-muscled, a bit of fat on his belly, tanned skin, usual for a sailor."

"Fat on the belly? Not long at sea, then." Halvar thought of the sparse diet on board ships that crossed the Storm Sea.

"As to that, I couldn't say. He wore a crux under his shirt, quite nice, gold." Dr. Moise pointed to the objects laid next to the body.

Halvar looked them over.

"Crux on a gold chain," he reported for Selim's notes. "Strings of white and purple wumpum. A few copper coins, Franchen-made. Nothing else? No purse?"

"This was all he had in his coat pockets. The rest we found in the woman's room."

"He was just stepping outside to relieve himself," Selim said. "He expected to go back to that woman."

Halvar nodded. "Good thought. He was taken by surprise. He didn't have a weapon, not even a small knife."

"Why the gold chain and crux?" Selim asked. "It's very fine, almost like something a woman would wear."

"Shows he's Roumi Rite Kristo," Halvar said. "Most Franchen are. No surprise there." He touched his own amulet. "It's a matter of faith, Selim, to carry a reminder of the Redeemer at all times. And he wouldn't put it off, not even for his, um, pleasure. One more reason to think this wasn't a robbery gone wrong. No Scavenger would leave that behind, Kristo or Islim."

"The coat is quite nice, too," Selim said, stroking the garment. "And the shirt is linen, fine-woven, good stitching. This Captain Girard liked to dress well. Look at that braid, and the gold buttons."

"Not quite gold," Halvar said, holding the coat closer to the lamp that hung from the ceiling beams. "This is gilt, a thin layer of paint over base metal. Girard wanted to make a show, but couldn't afford the real thing."

"Then he wasn't killed by a thief," Selim said. "They wouldn't be fooled by false gold."

"Maybe not," Halvar agreed. "But in the dim morning light, in the fog? I don't like to think it, but Flores

95

may be right about the Scavengers. He's been right before,"

"Possible, but not probable," Dr. Moise declared. "This wound was not made by the sort of knife carried by Scavengers. This was a very sharp, very narrow blade. And the one who wielded it knew exactly where to insert it. Scavengers tend to carry common daggers, and they go for the middle of the back, not the base of the neck."

"A professional assassin?" Halvar grimaced with frustration. "I thought we'd cleaned out their nest at the Mermaid Taberna. Don't tell me there's another one running loose on Manatas!"

"Then I won't tell you. I'll let you decide for yourself." Dr. Moise turned the body over, pointing to the narrow slot just under the dead man's skull. "I have not seen one such during my stay in Manatas, but in Corduva a man was brought in for autopsy after a fight in a taberna. The man was Franchen, an old soldier, the killer turned out to be one of his fellow Franchen, on their way to Afrika to take service with one or another of the Afrikan kings."

"I was approached by one of their commanders," Halvar said. "I refused his offer. I already had a job."

Selim frowned over her sketch.

"Not much blood," she commented.

"There wouldn't be," Dr. Moise told her. "The blade entered quite smoothly. No jagged edges."

"Well-kept, sharpened, ready for action." Halvar nodded. "An assassin's blade."

Dr. Moise nodded as well.

"One odd thing," he said. "I have used a straw to determine the angle of the stroke. Assuming that the man was killed while he was propped up against the wall of the crib, he would have his head down, so."

He demonstrated without opening his trousers. "If the assassin was taller than Girard, the stroke would be steep, angled downward. However, the stroke was shallow. The killer must have been as tall as Girard, but not much taller."

Halvar eyed the body.

"Not very tall, then. Middling height. Right or left hand?"

"I would say right," Dr. Moise answered.

"Mark that, Selim—killer of average height, right-handed."

"Like almost everyone in Manatas," Selim muttered as she wrote in her notebook.

There was a scuffle at the door. Zoltan thrust Michel Primero into the room.

"You wanted him, here he is."

Michel took one look at the body and cried out, "*Pie Chesu!* That is Captain Girard!"

"And that makes it official," Selim stated.

Halvar sighed deeply.

"Michel Primero, I have sad news. The four men that were left on the *Belle Fleur* are dead. I deeply regret that I killed one of them. The others were killed by the Locals when they attacked us. We gave full warning, tried to talk to them, but they seemed to think we were there to rob the ship. You'd better get someone over there before the storm hits."

Michel gasped, then swallowed hard.

"You said four. We left five on board. What about Jeannot, the ship's boy?"

"He's alive, safe, with friends," Halvar assured him. "You and I need to talk some more, Michel Primero. I want to know why Girard decided to sail in the middle of winter, why he came to Manatas, and who knew he was coming here."

"I already told you. He sailed because this Milord Summersby offered him a sack of silver to take him to Bella Mara. He put in here because he needed a safe harbor. As far as I know, no one knew he was coming."

"He sent no letter ahead, on one of the fishing boats out of West Caster?" Halvar tugged at his mustache.

"We didn't meet any such."

"Not even in Bos-Town?"

"We only stopped for supplies," Michel insisted. "We had to stay over a few extra days, to get Milady out of trouble, and to take on some kegs of rhum."

"What kind of trouble can anyone get into in Bos-Town?" Flores scoffed.

"Milady was arrested by their constabulary when she went for a stroll on the dock," Michel said with a grin. "They charged her with being too well-dressed."

"That's the Pure Sect for you," Donal said. "They're very strict about what gets worn, and by who."

"They said she was a whore," Michel said. "It cost Milord a silver imperial or two to get her out of their lockup. They were going to duck her in the river, to teach her humility."

"I don't think it would work," Halvar said. "I've met the lady."

Michel nodded. His grin faded.

"I'll have to send a crew across to the ship," he said. "We can't just let her ride loose. Even at anchor, you have to have someone on board."

"Do that," Halvar said. "But after the storm, if there is a storm, be prepared to answer some more questions."

"I've told you all I know," Michel said. "I have to get back to the ship. I'm the only one who can sail her, now that the captain is gone."

"Indeed? You're a navigator?"

Michel shrugged.

"I can follow a chart well enough, even if I can't make one. It's that passage into the bay that's tricky. I don't know the currents and shoals. Captain Girard was good at reading the water, like he was at reading the weather."

"If there is a storm brewing, you're better off on land," Donal said.

"Not so. I want to have a deck under my feet. When can I have the captain?" He turned to Dr. Moise.

"When I'm done with him," the Afrikan said.

"When the storm is past," Halvar decided. "We should have finished the investigation by then. As for your lad, he's in good hands, Heer Michel. Enjoy your stay on Manatas."

With that, Halvar led the way out to the courtyard. Dark clouds scudded overhead. Wind whistled through the gaps in the walls. Michel shivered, beckoned to his men, and scurried out the gates heading for the shelter of Maison Rouge.

"Storm's coming for sure," Donal remarked, with a glance at the rapidly approaching clouds. "I have to get back to Green Village, to make sure all is secured against the cold and wind."

"Not until we finish," Halvar said. "I'll need you nearby when Milord presents himself to Sultan Petrus. He should be along shortly, with Devallon at his heels. Keep watch for him and bring him to the sultan as soon as he gets here."

"What about us, Capitán?" Flores asked. "If there is a storm coming, the folk at the souk should be warned, too."

Halvar nodded.

"Tell Daoud the News-crier to put out the weather warning, then get yourself some food. You, too, Selim. Zoltan and Fergus, you two keep looking for that Afrikan, Ibo. He's got to be somewhere on the island.

"As for me, I've got my own report to make." Halvar surveyed the central tower of the Rabat. If the first confrontation with Milord Summersby had been bad, he suspected the next one would be even worse.

Sultan Petrus had to be told there was apparently yet another Franchen assassin loose in Manatas. And past experience told Halvar Sultan Petrus would not be pleased about it.

Chapter 13

HALVAR MOUNTED THE STAIRS TO THE SEC-
ond story of the tower where Sultan Petrus kept his
private quarters, just below Lady Ayesha's private
rooms and the harem. The peppery old soldier was
testy at the best of times. With winter coming on, his
old wounds ached, and the sultan was not one to suf-
fer in silence.

The Afrikan slave who attended him met Halvar
at the door. Halvar raised his eyebrows in silent question. The man answered with a grimace and a jerk of
the head.

"Something new inside," he said.

Sounds of hammering and metallic clangs made
Halvar's eyebrows rise yet another notch. He stepped
into the sultan's domain to find Malik the Smith over-
seeing the installation of an apparatus under one of the
windows that provided the sultan with a view of the

101

bay. It appeared to be a kind of covered brazier, held off the floor by four stout legs. A round pipe leading from the fire-pan was being attached to the outer bars of the window by one of Malik's Halfling apprentices, with much cursing in several languages..

"What do you think of that?" Sultan Petrus crowed as Malik and his two assistants wrestled with the thing.

"What is it?" Halvar asked.

"A stove! It's one of Leon di Vicenza's clever ideas."

Halvar nodded. "I saw something like it at the Gardens of Paradise. Fru Dani Glick has one."

"That was the first model. This one is better." The Sultan circled the thing, his silver-studded ivory peg thumping. "According to Malik, this will heat the room without filling it with smoke the way an open brazier does. As you see, it is smaller than those huge tiled things the Danes use that take up half a room. And there's a flat iron plate on the top where I can heat my mokka.

"Quite a useful thing, don't you think? Malik assures me he can make others. And once they see mine, others will want them. I can have Malik make another, and another. It will keep him busy during the winter months when other work is slack at the forge. I know an Afrikan who will pay a whole gold real to be warm this winter." He rubbed his hands in anticipation of revenue.

Halvar glanced at the Afrikan smith, but Malik appeared to be too intent on placing the new stove in the exact spot where it would be most effective to react to the sultan's gloating. Presumably, some of that money earned by the sale of the smith's labor would be put aside for the calif's tolls, but most would go to Sultan Petrus's personal treasure chest. It was highly unlikely Malik would see any of it.

"How does it work?" Halvar asked.

He had grown up with the vast tiled stoves of the Dane-March, but this was smaller, more compact, almost portable. *Something like this could be carried by an army on the move*, he thought. And if you could get it hot enough to cook on, the possibilities were staggering.

Old Sergeant Olaf always said that an army moved its stomach. More than one campaign had failed because the soldiers were starving too far from their supply lines. If they could be well-fed on the march, they would move faster and be ready for action at any time. Even a lowly pikeman like him could see that.

"How does it work?" he asked, circling the thing.

"The fire is inside here." Malik demonstrated. "The smoke goes into this pipe and out the window. The trick is to keep air going into the stove, through this grate on the bottom. There is a pan of sand underneath to catch the embers, so as not to set the floor on fire."

"Clever," Halvar commented. "But it would be, if Leon devised it." He turned to the sultan. "Any hope of getting him out of that fratery?"

Sultan Petrus sighed and sank into his favorite chair, which had been moved close to the new stove.

"Abbas Mikhail has refused all requests to 'remove Frater Leonides from his guiding hand,' as he puts it. He's even allowed some of Leon's old students to come to the fratery, so that Leon can resume his lectures, rather than allow him to come into Manatas."

"So, the Seekers of Truth are back at their lessons," Halvar said. "I hope they find what they're seeking. There's little enough truth in this world."

"The Holy Book should be enough for them," the sultan snapped.

The Afrikan servant darted forward with a footstool on which the sultan could prop up his ivory peg.

103

"So, Hireling, what's this I hear about a murder on the waterfront? I thought the Town Guard was supposed to keep things quiet. One sailor sticks a knife into another sailor, that's not a murder. That's just sailors fighting over a woman. Or a game of dice."

"Not sailors, and not a game of dice. Although there may be a woman at the bottom of this," Halvar conceded. "The dead man is Captain Franz Girard. Franchen. That's his round ship in the harbor. He came ashore yesterday, just around nightfall, too late to contact the tally-man. I suppose he was going to do it today, but someone stuck him with a very thin, sharp blade before he could do so."

"Nasty," was the sultan's opinion. "Who did it?"

"That is what we have yet to find out," Halvar admitted. "The guards who keep order on the waterfront thought at first it was a Scavenger, but I don't think so. Not Emir Achmet's style at all. His people do their dirty work in the souk, they stay away from the waterfront, except for the Afrikan who tends to the public latrine.

"Besides, a Scavenger would never have left a gold chain and crux on the body. Tenente Flores thinks it's one of the ship's crew, but they don't have the right kind of blades. Nor would they want to kill the one person who could get them out of this harbor. From what I heard, only their captain had the skill to do that."

Sultan Petrus eased his ivory leg into a more comfortable position.

"You've spoken to this crew?"

"I spoke with their leader. I'll have more to say to him later. What you should know, Excellent Sultan, is that Captain Girard was taking passengers from Kibbick to Bella Mara, in Sultan Calvera's territory." Halvar paused, then added, "I've told the passengers, a Bretain milord and milady, to present themselves to you as soon as they are settled. I thought you should take a good look at them before sending them on their way to Bella Mara."

"Aha!" Sultan Petrus rifled around in the papers stacked on the small table beside his great armchair. "Bella Mara, is it? I've got letters from my son. He and Don Felipe, may he rule long, are staying in Bella Mara for the Nativity celebrations. They say the festivities are quite elaborate in Roumi Rite chapels, much singing and feasting. Which reminds me, Don Alvaro, you must come to my End-of-Fast celebration tomorrow."

"It will be my pleasure," Halvar said, his heart sinking. It would not be pleasant to sit with people who spoke only Arabi, laced with allusions to things he did not know, in accents he barely understood, eating heavily spiced food that would not sit well on his stomach. However, if this is what being capitán of the Town Guards entailed, he would put on his finest Andalusian jacket and attend this dinner.

"How is Don Felipe's tour of Al-Andalus-in-Exile going?" Halvar asked. He tried not to let jealousy put the edge to his tone. He should have been the one to accompany Don Felipe instead of sitting on this island, training raw recruits in basic military practices and trying to keep order in this rowdy settlement.

Don Roderigo ibn Petrus had taken his place at the calif's right hand. Halvar reminded himself that he was, after all, only a hireling, that the calif had every right to choose his own companions, and that he was doing an important job in Manatas. He still felt that he, not Roderigo, should be at Don Felipe's back.

Petrus continued grumbling as he looked through the papers.

"According to the official report, our calif is doing very well. He was well-received by Sultan Pennina in

Salaamabad, where he started the Fasting Month before going on to Terra Mara. He spoke with the Local sachems and visited several towns established by Oropans of various Kristo sects. The harvest went well, there is plenty stored for the winter."

"But?" Halvar heard the hesitation in the sultan's voice.

"My son, Roderigo, has written in cypher. He's like his mother, devious. According to him, there are divisions among the Oropans, mostly about the use of Afrikan slave labor. The Oropans who grow food are generous to their Afrikans, allow them to attend the muskat if they are Islim, see that they are allotted a portion of what they grow.

"Those who are growing tabac for sale in Oropa are more vicious, treat their Afrikans like animals, do not allow them good rations and provide minimal housing, if any. They also forbid them to follow Islim, or any other religion."

"Foolish," Halvar commented. "You can't expect starving men to work well."

"Precisely what Don Felipe told them," Sultan Petrus said. "But Oropans, particularly Bretains, are stubborn and greedy. There was some trouble about this."

He consulted another paper.

"Don Felipe, may he reign long, and my son Roderigo are now in Bella Mara with Sultan Calvera, whose territory is right next to the Ashanti. More and more Afrikans coming in, most of them slaves."

Halvar tugged at his mustache.

"I see where you're going. Who is bringing these slaves to Nova Mundum? And more to the point, who is profiting by it?"

"It's not my problem," Sultan Petrus said, tossing the paper back onto the table. "I'm more worried about being taken by surprise from the north.

"The Bretains in West Caster are always trying to push farther west, over the mountains, but the Mahak stand firm and won't allow it. So, they try to get into Andalusian territory through the back door, so to speak, getting concessions to mine rocks and coals in Sequan-nok.

"Peninna's so taken up with his religious practices, he can't see what's going on under his nose. And then the Huron come south during the cold months, when the river that separates their territory from West Caster freezes over. They sneak across it, say they're hunt-ing deer. Hah!" Petrus barked a mirthless laugh, then turned back to Halvar.

"What's your opinion of this Franchen sea captain coming here? I'm not being an old woman seeing Fran-chen spies under the bed, am I? There's a forest and a mountain range between the Huron and us, but they and the Franchen are still too close for my comfort. I don't want another assassin in Manatas."

"You may not want one, Excellent Sultan, but it appears you've got one. Dr. Moise concurs with me. This murder was done by someone with a good deal of experience. He knew where the captain was, he wait-ed for his victim to finish what he was doing with his whore, and he struck when Girard was most vulnera-ble, when he had his trousers open to piss."

"And who is this assassin?" the sultan demanded.

"I'm not sure," Halvar said slowly. "He could have been staying here in Manatas, waiting for Girard to ap-pear. Girard sent a message to someone before he went off to pleasure himself, so someone in Manatas knew him. We don't know what the message was about, or who was supposed to get it, or if it was even delivered."

"That doesn't make me any happier."

"Of course, the murderer could have been on the ship with the captain, waiting for a chance to kill him in a place like Manatas," Halvar went on. "There were two swordsmen aboard the *Belle Fleur*—a Bretain milord and his so-called bodyguard, a Franchen mercenary."

"Mercenary, eh?" Sultan Petrus frowned. "One of your old companions?"

"No companion of mine, but I met him, a long time ago. "

Voices on the stairs outside the door drew their attention.

"It appears you are about to meet him, too, Excellent Sultan."

Sultat Petrus waved the workmen into a corner, arranged his robes and turban, and prepared to greet his newly-arrived guests. Halvar moved toward the door.

"Stay here, Don Alvaro," Petrus ordered. "If these are Franchen or Bretains, I may need an interpreter."

Halvar recognized another voice, carrying over the other two.

"I believe an able interpreter has invited herself to this party," he said with a wry smile.

"Milord Summersby and Milady Summersby and their attendant, Musket-man Devallon, wish an audience with the Sultan of Manatas." the attendant at the door announced.

"Show them in." Sultan Petrus said, grandly.

Halvar took his place next to the sultan's chair. If he couldn't be next to the calif, at least he was close to the calif's representative in Manatas.

Chapter 14

MILORD SUMMERSBY SWEPT INTO THE CHAM-
ber, followed by Devallon and Milady. Selim scrambled after them and salaamed hastily to her father.

"I know some Franchen," she explained in response
to Petrus's questioning eyebrow. "And Capitán Don Alvaro always wants me to take notes on what's said and
done in interviews."

"Sit there, and don't speak unless I tell you to," Halvar ordered, pointing to the small table which already
held the sultan's favorite mokka service. He turned to
the sultan. "Excellent Sultan, may I present Milord and
Milady Summersby, late of Kibbick. And their attendant,
Heer Musket-man Devallon."

For his audience, Milord had chosen a pale-green
coat, open to reveal a silk waistcoat and lace-trimmed
linen shirt. His breeches were fitted to display his legs,
his shoes had glittering buckles, and he wore a broad-

brimmed Franchen hat trimmed with a magnificent pink plume from some exotic bird of Afrika. A slender sword hung from his belt in a fine leather scabbard.

Devallon had changed his shabby leather jacket for one with silver tips to the laces that held it closed across his broad chest. His hat was also broad-brimmed, trimmed with a plain spray of goose feathers instead of an extravagant plume. His sword, however, was in a plain leather sheath. Clearly, his weapon was meant for use, not show.

Both men were eclipsed by Milady Summersby's magnificence. Her gown was of rose-colored silk, cut low enough in the bodice to reveal more of her bosom than Halvar thought necessary, given the chilly wind blowing through the island. The full skirt was caught up with ribbons to reveal a quilted and embroidered underskirt. Her waist had been cinched to make it small, and her breasts threatened to burst over the low neckline.

Her pale-blond hair was piled atop her head and secured with jeweled pins, except for one curl that had been artfully draped onto her neck. Her only concession to the weather was a long stole of fox furs, which she wore over her arms instead of huddling into it as any sensible woman would do. She had exaggerated the arch of her eyebrows with a dark pencil and reddened her lips as well.

Halvar's eyes widened as he took in Milady's attire, then narrowed as he realized the extent of her major solecism. She had not covered her hair!

It was a stunning breach of Islim etiquette. Every woman over the age of puberty in Manatas covered her hair. If they were Islim, they wore a hijab, the scarf that covered everything except the face, and often wore a full burka when they went out in public. Oropan wo-

men wore caps that varied according to their national-
ity, from the plain starched white ones of the Pure Sect
Kristos to the lace-trimmed items favored by Franchen
and Danic merchant's wives. Yehudit women wore col-
orful kerchiefs and caps that tied under their chins. Afrikans had elaborately tied head-cloths that indicated
not only their rank but their tribe as well.

Even the whores on Maiden Lane covered their hair
with thin kutton or silk scarves when they went out of
doors. Only the Locals, mostly Algonkin, wore no cap
or hat, but they secured their braided hair with leather
thongs that could, by extension, be considered head
coverings.

Sultan Petrus gasped at the sight. Selim giggled as
she realized Milady's mistake. For her part, Milady Summersby seemed totally unaware of what she had done.
She smiled directly at the sultan, who harumphed and
looked away from the enticing sight,

Both men bowed in the Franchen style, one leg
forward, one leg behind. Milady curtsied, revealing yet
more bosom.

"*Salaam aleikum*, Excellent Sultan," Devallon began
in careful Arabi. "Forgive us for being so forward, but
Capitán Halvar Danske told us to address you as soon
as we could.

"Milord and Milady Summersby beg your permission to remain here in Manatas until such time as their
ship can continue on its journey. The commander and
navigator, Captain Girard, has met with an unfortunate
accident, and they must stay on Manatas until he can
be replaced."

"Accident?" Petrus said. "According to my Capitán
of Guards, Don Alvaro Danico, he's been murdered.
A knife in the back of the head, no less!" He glared at
the Bretains. "What do you know about that?"

111

Milord and Devallon consulted in Franchen while Milady stared at the exotic tapestries, the silk cushions, and inlaid tables set around the room.

"We know nothing of the matter, except as much as your captain has told us," Devallon said smoothly. "We are here in Manatas purely by chance. We came to inform you of our presence as a matter of courtesy, before continuing to Terra Mara."

Milady interrupted Devallon's diplomatic speech.

"I'm here to see your lady," she announced.

Sultan Petrus looked startled at being directly addressed by this brazen woman. He cleared his throat.

"Hem! Lady Ayesha does not receive casual visitors," he began.

Selim scrambled to her feet.

"Perhaps she'd like some company," she said. She shot Halvar a mischievous glance. "If I may, Honored Father, I can show this lady to the harem to meet with Ayesha. It will amuse her. She can practice her Franchen and show off Baby Zuzu."

Before Sultan Petrus could object, Selim had taken Milady in charge and hurried her out the door and onto the stairs to the third floor and the harem, the forbidden women's chambers permitted only to females and eunuchs.

"I beg pardon for Milady Summersby's behavior," Devallon said as soon as the two were safely out of earshot. "Milady isn't used to Andalusian ways. Franchen and Bretain women have a good deal more freedom of movement and speech than those of Al-Andalus."

"Tell her that if she's going to stay in Manatas, she'd better learn to cover her hair," Halvar said. "It's the custom here."

"I hope she doesn't expect Lady Ayesha to accompany her around Manatas," Petrus grumbled. "Lady

Ayesha has recently given birth and is still delicate." He clapped his hands, and the doorkeeper appeared. "Mokka!"

Halvar's eyebrows rose. He didn't want to remind the sultan in front of others that it was still the Fasting Month, when food and drink were forbidden to Islim between sunrise and sunset.

Sultan Petrus harumphed, guessing what Halvar was thinking.

"Not as food or drink," he said, "but as a matter of courtesy. And for medicinal purposes. Dr. Moise has informed me that mokka is good for the heart."

"With respect, Excellent Sultan, we have no time for mokka," Devallon said. "Milord must find someone who can take the ship *Belle Fleur* to its intended destination."

A squad of servants marched in with a brass pot of hot mokka and several cups, all of which were ceremoniously deposited on the small table and the used cups quickly removed.

"Sit!" Sultan Petrus ordered. "And tell me where were you planning to go, if not Manatas?"

Devallon and Summersby looked around for chairs. Halvar remained standing, but the two visitors had no choice but to sit on the cushions offered by the servants, an awkward business for men in boots who had swords at their hips.

Mokka was poured and served. Halvar had grown used to the bittersweet taste of the brewed beans flavored with honey and cinnamon that Sultan Petrus imbibed nonstop during the day, but Milord's face twisted at the taste. Devallon took one sip and put his cup down quickly.

"We are bound for Sultan Calvera's territory, where Milord has a legacy waiting," Devallon explained. "If I

113

may speak in Erse?" He looked anxiously from the sultan to Halvar. "Arabi is not natural to me, I am more fluent in Erse, as is your noble captain."

Sultan Petrus nodded. "I understand Erse, Musketman. Continue, if you will. What business brings Milord to Nova Mundum at this time of the year? It is not the time for the feria, and the winter storms are fierce."

Devallon consulted with Milord again in Franchen. Halvar strained, but was only able to catch a word here and there: *land...tabac...Milady.*

Devallon took another sip of mokka.

"It is this way. Milord Summersby received word there is a legacy waiting for him in Sultan Calvera's territory, a farm where tabac is grown to be sent to Franchenland and Bretain, where they will pay well for it. He has been traveling for several months to take possession of this land, sailing first from Bretain to Franchenland, and from there to Kibbick.

"In Kibbick, he hired the ship *Belle Fleur* and its captain to take him to Bella Mara. He will swear on any saint you like, and on the Redeemer's own salvation, that he had no knowledge of Captain Girard before he set foot in Kibbick this summer."

Halvar turned to the sultan.

"I think Girard was the one who brought the Afrikan Ochiye Aboutiye from Savana Port to Manatas for the Spring Feria. As far as I can find out, neither he nor his ship came to Manatas after that," he said in Arabi.

"I expect he went back to Franchenland after the feria, with the winter furs and timber," Petrus said. "I don't know why he'd go back to Kibbick. Most of the trade goes south, to Afrika."

Devallon coughed meaningfully.

"Ahem! I was on *Belle Fleur* when it left Franchenland in Julius month of this year. Captain Girard had fitted it out for passengers. He had aboard twenty-five young women, bound for Kibbick at the orders of Lovis the Younger, the son of Imperator Lovis.

"It is Lovis the Younger's belief that the soldiers and traders in Kibbick are being distracted from their duty by their Huron wives. The Franchen women were supposed to remind them of who and what they are, and to whom they owe their allegiance. They were provided with good dowries to make them more attractive to the Franchen of Kibbick."

"Was Milady Summersby one of those?" Halvar asked with a wry twist of the mouth. He had a good idea of the sort of women who would be shipped over to Nova Mundum as brides for soldiers, farmers and trappers. "I assume she was not intended for Milord when she sailed."

Devallon let his smile answer for him.

"Milord was already in Kibbick, looking for a way to get south, when the ladies arrived. Of course he picked the prettiest one for himself. As for Captain Girard, he was ready to winter over in Kibbick. No one wanted to sail, what with the weather and the possibility of being boarded by pirates."

"Pirates!" Sultan Petrus exploded into an Arabi rant. "That's all we need! Pirates! Let them stay in the Mechican Sea! Afrikans, Mechicans, and who knows who else! They lurk in the inlets around the Pizzle, they grab what they can, and they wave letters of marque that they say give them the right to interrupt shipping of enemies. Except that Lovis Younger seems to have taken his father's orders too far and has declared war on everyone!"

"Which brings us back to Captain Girard." Halvar switched from Arabi to Erse again. "Milord Summersby, what were your relations with the captain?"

"Relations?" Milord had been trying to follow the various conversations while staring into his mokka. "We had no relations. He was paid to sail his ship from Kibbick to BelMar. He insisted on following the coastline of West Caster, claimed he was trying to avoid some current that would take us north and east instead of south and west."

"He didn't follow your orders?"

"He did not! He dawdled! He took us to Bos-Town, where my wife was insulted and jailed!" Milord puffed indignantly. "And then he said the weather was going to turn nasty, and we had to go to Manatas, of all places, to ride out the storm. There's no storm that I can see, just this infernal sleet."

Halvar thought this over.

"There were no incidents on board the ship? Girard seems to have had a reputation as a lover of women. Did he make advances to Milady that were, um, unwelcome?"

"Milady was unwell for much of the voyage," Milord said stiffly. "I, of course, am an excellent sailor. Sieur Devallon and I were able to use the time to perfect our swordsmanship."

"Always a good idea," Halvar murmured, eying the rapier that hung at Devallon's side. He had a good idea who benefited the most from those exercises.

"So, Excellent Sultan, you see that we are here by chance, not choice, and that we must remain until the weather clears." Devallon said briskly, "And there is one more small matter that I would bring to the attention of the Excellent Sultan.

"At present, Milord and Milady Summersby are housed in a small cottage near the waterfront, formerly occupied by tavern keepers. It is quite inadequate to their needs, and insulting to their position. Might there

there some way they can be better accommodated? Some house not being used at present where they may stay until another navigator is found and they can continue on their journey?

"It is my understanding that several of the large villas along the Broad Way are empty during the winter months, since their owners go south into Afrikan territory where the weather is less rigorous."

Halvar thought of those large villas in the sector between the Broad Way and the Great River. It was true they stood empty while their owners spent the winter months in more favorable climes. Would the sultan summarily donate one of these to the visiting dignitaries?

Sultan Petrus frowned at the Bretain.

"The houses of the Afrikan merchants are theirs. I can hardly quarter guests on them without their consent. You may remain in the house formerly used by the Taverniers, which owes its rent directly to the Manatas Town treasury. I understand it is furnished in the Oropan style, so it should be quite comfortable enough for your needs.

"As for your other problem, I suggest you apply at the madrassa for someone who has studied navigation. It is possible one of the students or teachers there will be able to get you where you want to go. *Salaam aleikum*, Milord Summersby. Ah, here is Milady!"

Milady Summersby appeared at the door, looking distressed.

"We have to get out of here!" she announced in shrill Franchen, sure that no one would understand her. "I can't stay here a minute longer!"

Milord smiled weakly and bowed once again to the sultan, then followed his wife down the stairs.

117

Devallon sighed.

"You see how it is," he told Halvar in Erse. "A Hireling's work is never done, is it?"

"Meet me at the Mermaid Taberna after evening prayers," Halvar invited him. "We can have a good, long talk, Musket-man, and you can tell me what really went on on that ship!"

"I hope the food there is better than the slop served at La Maison Rouge," Devallon muttered over his shoulder as he followed his employer down the stair to the courtyard below.

Chapter 15

"PHEW!" SULTAN PETRUS LET OUT A LONG, exasperated breath. Halvar poured another cup of mokka, handed it to him, and took one for himself as well.

"Here, Excellent Sultan, that should take the taste of those Oropans out of your mouth."

The sultan sipped greedily.

"What do you make of their tale, Don Alvaro?"

"It hangs true, as far as it goes," Halvar said slowly. "Michel Primero, the ship's steersman, said they had a cargo of women from Franchenland. Providing Franchen women for his men, that sounds like Lovis the Younger. The Imperator's getting older, he's letting his sons have some license. One of them's taken hold in Al-Andalus, is calling it Hispania and establishing the Roumi Rite, changing muskats into chapels."

"And forcing anyone who won't take the water to choose between a ship and the fire," Sultan Petrus grumbled. "Not a pleasant choice. Especially for Yehudit. Islim can go to Afrika. Yehudit aren't welcome there."

Selim popped back into the room.

"Milady Summersby is giving her man an earful!" she reported. "I don't know all the Franchen words she used, but I don't think they're very polite. You can hear her clear across the courtyard."

"What do you make of her?" Halvar asked.

"I've never seen anything like!" Selim said. "She was all smiles, but the smile didn't reach her eyes. She said how nice Baby Zuzu was, but she sort-of flinched to see that Baby Zuzu was being fed by a Local woman. And her eyes really opened when she saw Maya.

"Ayesha tried to make conversation in Franchen, but it's been a while since we had lessons with Leon, and Ayesha had forgotten most of what we learned. It was things like, 'Welcome to Manatas' and 'The air is cold today' and 'This is my baby Zulaika, whom we call Zuzu.' I don't think Milady Summersby was impressed by Lady Ayesha, not at all."

"And what about you? Were you impressed by Milady Summersby?"

Selim's heavy brows met over her snub nose in a frown.

"She wears too many jewels, and she doesn't cover her hair. She stinks of heavy perfume. And she thinks she's finer than anyone else."

"All this from one meeting?" Sultan Petrus sounded skeptical.

"You can tell how someone feels by the way they treat people," Selim said. "Milady Summersby ignored me, fawned over Ayesha, flinched every time Star-Bright or Maya came close. She fears Locals. And she's not too happy with Afrikans, either, I could tell. She shifted her skirts so they didn't touch when Ada and Zara came near."

"In short, she's a typical Franchen woman," Halvar summed up. "Probably never seen anyone but Oropans until she took ship for Nova Mundum."

"Why come here, then?" Selim wondered.

"That's a tale for her to tell," Halvar said. "But I've seen the woman who escorted her to Nova Mundum, and I have a few ideas about her intentions." And they didn't include marriage, he added, silently.

The Afrikan doorkeeper announced, "The Commission on Women has arrived, Excellent Sultan."

Eva Hakim and Dani Glick marched into the chamber. Eva Hakim greeted the sultan and presented a roll of paper.

"*Salaam aleikum*, Sultan Petrus. We have concluded our task. The women of Maiden Lane have all been examined." Her thin lips tightened in an expression of distaste. "Not all willingly, but thoroughly."

"Now may I get back to my own business?" Dani asked. "It's nearly dark, and I have to get back to the Gardens of Paradise to light the lamps for the Festival of Lights."

"Not staying here, in the Yehudit Quarter?" Halvar teased her.

"There are more festivities in Green Village," Dani retorted. "In fact, I was going to invite the Excellent Sultan to partake of our Festival feast, where we re-enact the great battles between the Yehudit and the Old Greco forces. And, as such things sometimes happen, it's also the day of Nativity, so there will be a double ceremony."

Eva Hakim sniffed. "The Prophet said to respect the other Peoples of the Book. He did not condone joining them in their heretical celebrations."

"But it would be good politics," Halvar reminded the sultan. "And I'm sure Lady Ayesha would enjoy a day of festivity away from the Rabat."

"You may inform the good people of Green Village that I will attend the festivities," Sultan Petrus declared. "With Lady Ayesha. Unfortunately, Baby Zuzu is too young to enjoy such things, and the cold may not be good for her, but my…son, Selim, will also attend."

"Unless I'm on duty with Capitán Don Alvaro," Selim muttered.

"Fru Glick, Eva Hakim, did you notice the woman in the courtyard when you came into the tower?" Halvar asked.

"How could we not!" Eva Hakim's face twisted in distaste. "A spectacle of extravagance! What sort of woman goes about decked in furs with her hair unbound and uncovered? Even the poor creatures of Maiden Lane show more respect for Ilha, may his name be blessed, and the Prophet, may his name be praised."

Dani Glick was more tolerant.

"Courtesan, I'd say. Franchen, from what I heard. A whore, but a very expensive one. What's she doing here?"

"She came on the *Belle Fleur*, that round ship in the harbor," Halvar said. "With a Bretain, Milord Summersby. He calls her Milady, says she's his wife.

"If she isn't, he's in trouble," Dani said with a knowing smile. "She's in a rare temper, not happy to be in Manatas at all. I heard her giving him what-for all the way to the gate. He fair ran ahead of her while she nagged at him all the way down to Pearl Street."

"She may not be pleased, but here she'll stay until they can find someone to get that round ship out of the bay," Halvar said. He turned to the sultan. "Is there a vacant villa that can house those two and their servants until such time as they can leave?"

"I won't pander to their self-importance," Sultan Petrus growled. "They're where I can find them—on Pearl

Street, in the Oropan houses. I don't want them any-where else, certainly not here in the Rabat. Let them stay near the waterfront—and keep an eye on them. Set one of the guards to watch them. I don't trust Fran-chen."

"Especially not when one of them may well be a murderer," Halvar said.

"Which one?" Dani asked.

"And why?" Selim added.

"I leave these matters to you, Don Alvaro," Eva Hakim said. "I shall return to the House of the Green Crescent. We are ending our Fasting Month tomorrow. I shall attend Lady Ayesha's End-of-Fast feast tomor-row, Excellent Sultan. *Salaam aleikum!*"

When she'd left, the atmosphere in the chamber seemed to lighten. Halvar turned to Dani Glick.

"You seem to be familiar with Milady's sort of wo-man."

"I've met a few," Dani admitted. "In Oropa, before Mauritz got his grand idea of sailing to Nova Mundum."

"Courtesan, you said."

"Not exactly a whore," Dani explained. "More of a concubine, if you take my meaning. Good enough to be allowed into a noble household, not good enough for formal marriage."

"She was one of Lovis Younger's brides for sol-diers," Selim put in.

"And she wound up with a milord. Not bad," Dani said.

"And they took ship from Kibbick to Terra Mara," Sultan Petrus said.

"Where no one knows them," Halvar added. "Which raises a good question. Are these two who they say they are? And if not, who are they? And is one of them the Franchen assassin we're looking for?"

"A woman assassin?" Sultan Petrus shook his head. "Not likely."

Dani Glick smiled nastily.

"Anything is possible, Excellent Sultan. Especially in Manatas."

Halvar said, "Whoever killed Captain Girard waited behind the whore's crib and smoked a pipe of tabac. That's not something a Franchen woman would do. I think we can eliminate Milady from our list of suspects in this murder."

"That leaves Milord and Devallon," Selim said.

"And their servants. Don't ever forget their servants," Halvar warned. "Remember that so-called vizier? Servants have their own plots and plans, not always for the good of their masters."

Sultan Petrus shifted uneasily in his chair.

"Fru Glick, I thank you for your information, and for your service on Maiden Lane. If you wish to take your leave and return to your place of entertainment, you may do so. I accept your invitation to the Festival of Lights celebrations in three days, on behalf of myself and my children and wife."

Dani bowed and skipped out, leaving Halvar to face the sultan and Selim.

"We still have a problem," he said. "The Afrikan named Ibo is still missing. I fear for him, Excellent Sultan. More than that, I feel that if he is not found, and quickly, there will be trouble with the Scavengers. Emir Achmet has been willing to curb his men, but they can become a violent mob if provoked. A needless death, unavenged, may set them off."

"Then get Flores and his men to work harder. I've got enough to worry about without having a horde of beggars and lowlifes raging through the streets of Manatas."

Halvar bowed and let himself out, with Selim close behind him. He paused on the landing. She bumped into him, and the two staggered down the stairs, nearly in each other's arms.

Once steady, Halvar gently pushed Selim away. The girl tried to cling to his arm, but he firmly set her back into the doorway.

"It's getting dark," he said. "You'd best go back inside."

"But there's still work to be done, Don Alvaro," she insisted, clearly longing to accompany him to his dinner at the Mermaid Taberna.

"Not tonight. For now, dine with your stepmother and father. Be nice to Baby Zuzu. Check those lesson-books Leon gave you and practice your Franchen, And see what you can make of that journal of Girard's. It might have a clue as to what he was up to and why he came to Manatas in the first place. Maybe even the name of the mysterious person who was waiting for him.

"I'm going to have a chat with an old comrade, of sorts. Musket-man Devallon has a few tales to tell, if I'm not mistaken, and he's more likely to tell them to me if there's no one else listening. I'll let you know what he says tomorrow morning," he added as Selim's eyebrows met over her nose in her customary pout.

With that, Halvar left his disciple almost in tears. His manner had been brutal, but he had to nip this hero-worship in the bud before the girl fancied herself in love with him. A hearty meal, a game of tables, and a long talk awaited him at the Mermaid Taberna, and he was looking forward to a good, long rest after a day of adventure. He only hoped he'd get it.

Chapter 16

HALVAR STEPPED INTO THE COURTYARD OF the Rabat and looked for a guardsman to carry the lantern as he made his way back to the waterfront and the conviviality of the Mermaid Taberna. The candles had been lit, and the courtyard was buzzing with the coming and going of the changing shifts of guards. Halvar had divided the small squad into three patrols, so that Manatas would be guarded even when most of the world was asleep.

Tenente Flores stood at the gate, nodding to his men as they passed by.

"How goes it, Tenente?" Halvar greeted him. "Have they found Ibo yet?"

"Not a sign of him," Flores grumbled. "What do you think, Capitán? Has he fled Manatas altogether?"

"I think we're too late," Halvar said. "If we're dealing with a professional assassin, he won't want any witnesses."

"Tcha!" Flores clicked his tongue in exasperation. Then he saw the donkey cart at the gate. "More trouble, Capitan. Look who's come to call on the sultan!"

From the smell of it, the cart was the one used by Ibo to carry his odoriferous burden to the Scavenger's Pits, where it would be deposited for use in the tannery up-the-hills, out of the way of more genteel inhabitants of Manatas. Its passengers and escort were no less aromatic, and even less acceptable, in Halvar's opinion.

Emir Achmet, the leader of the Scavengers, sat within the cart, wrapped in a mismatched set of fur pelts over his patched caftan. His head was topped by a turban pinned with a gaudy brooch. Walking beside the cart, with heavy wool robes over their ragged caftans, were his two lieutenants, Rachev and Osman.

Achmet eyed Halvar with disdain.

"*Aleikum salaam*, Capitán Don Alvaro. It seems you have not been told of our custom of almsgiving at the end of the Fasting Month."

"Almsgiving is a requirement of the Prophet," Rachev added piously. "And the Redeemer also encouraged folk to be generous, especially at the time of his Nativity."

"So, Don Alvaro, since you haven't been around to do what's right, we've come to remind you." Osman smiled at Halvar, showing his few broken teeth.

"Our late lamented friend, Tenente Gomez, was always most generous." Achmet eyed Halvar warily. "Tenente Gomez and I had a certain…understanding."

Halvar took a deep breath and wished he hadn't. Faithful Islim they might be, but they hadn't obeyed the strictures about using the *hammam* before prayer in a very long time.

As for Gomez and his "understandings," he had a good idea of what that entailed. Gomez had looked the other way while Achmet's men robbed small shop-keepers and plundered goods in warehouses, then insisted on taking a share of the profits of whatever sales there were. If Achmet hadn't gotten the message that Halvar wouldn't play that game, now was the time to make it absolutely clear.

"Noble Emir," he said, "I regret not giving you the alms you so richly deserve, but there are matters that must be attended to. Whatever understanding you had with my predecessor died with him. However, I will certainly make sure you get what is coming to you, as soon as I have the time."

"You mean, after you find out who killed the dead Franchen?"

"Tenente Flores thinks it's one of your people."

Flores scowled at the Emir.

"All we have to do is round them up, question them hard. They'll talk."

"I disagree with Tenente Flores," Halvar said. "For one thing, your man Ibo is still missing."

Achmet's voice was sharp. "Haven't you found him yet, Flores? You've been all over the souk, interrupting business."

"We are looking for him. We'll find him."

"If he's alive," Osman said. "Ibo does what you tell him to. He's always back by midday. His cart came back without him. I don't think he'd let the donkey go free if he was still alive."

"And if he's not, who cares?" Rachev stepped forward, hand on the knife at his belt. "After all, he's just a poor Afrikan, and one who cleaned latrines, at that. Not important enough for the Manatas Town Guard to move their lazy arses to protect."

Flores started to move towards Rachev, bludgeon in hand. Halvar stepped between them.

128

"In the eyes of both the Prophet and the Redeemer, all souls are equal," he pronounced. "And I swore to keep Manatas safe for the Calif Don Felipe, may he live long, What's more, I want to talk to that Afrikan myself. I think he may have seen the murderer, if not the murder."

"If you don't find the killer, we will," Rachev promised, glaring at Flores.

"And we won't wait until spring, and the Grand Divan at the feria to take care of him," Osman added.

"That you will not!" Halvar said. "There will be justice done, but under the law. So says the calif, and so it will be done!"

"And the alms?" Achmet's oily voice cut through the argument.

"There will be a suitable donation to the Scavengers from the sultan, I am sure," Halvar said.

"And from yourself?" Achmet hinted.

"I am a stranger to Manatas. I'm not familiar with the customary amount." Halvar smiled blandly, mentally calculating how much this old thief would demand, and how much he could bargain down. "Are you not compensated by the town treasury for your services in keeping the streets clean of filth?"

"A mere pittance." Achmet waved one hand, showing off a large ring with a red stone of dubious origin. "When you consider the difficulties of the task, and the unpleasantness should my people fail in their duty. Manatas would be covered with dung and debris in a few days if my people didn't go through the streets and alleys.

"And Mullah Abadul himself has praised us for allowing the Faithful of Islim the opportunity to fulfill the commandments of giving alms to the poor."

"True." *And your nimble-fingered youths just happen to pick up small items from the stands at the souk, to be resold in Green Village*, Halvar added silently. *Not to mention the other things, not so small, that will get lifted from vacant houses or warehouses if my guards aren't vigilant.*

"I will visit you at the Scavengers Pit as soon as I have found the assassin," he said aloud. "I wish you the joys of this festive season, when Islim, Kristo and Yehudit celebrate together."

"And we'll let you know as soon as we find Ibo," Flores added as the driver started to turn the cart around.

Halvar stopped the procession.

"One moment. Rachev, Osman...what do you know of Ibo? I see him every day, he's very diligent, but does he really know what he's about?"

Rachev shrugged.

"He's a halfwit. I think something frightened him badly when he was a sprout. He's not much for chat, doesn't know much Arabi."

"I think he was one of those souls kidnapped in Afrika, brought here by ship," Osman put in. "He had some flogging scars on his back. And he didn't hear well, either. You had to say things twice and three times before he could understand."

"But once he did understand, he did what he was told," Rachev concluded.

"So, if he saw something, who would he tell about it?" Halvar frowned and tugged at his mustache. A picture was forming in his mind, not a good one.

"Me, I guess," Osman said slowly. "I sort of got along with him. I'm a bit slow myself, you see. Rachev's got the wit between us. I'm the one put Ibo on the waterfront latrine detail, and he comes to me for advice when he needs it."

Halvar turned to Flores.

"Come with me to the waterfront, and then go over every inch of alley. Check those spaces between the warehouses. And has anyone checked the latrine?"

Flores's dark face paled.

"We looked inside, first thing. Didn't see him there, so we went on to other places."

"Did you go *into* the latrine?"

"You mean, all the ways in? Um, no."

"Do it," Halvar snapped. He beckoned to the nearest guardsman. "Get a lantern and follow us. I have a very bad feeling about this."

Emir Achmet's usual bland smile had turned to a scowl.

"If anything has happened to that poor Afrikan, I will not rest until he is avenged. I take care of my people, as a good emir should."

"And I take care of Manatas," Halvar reminded him.

The lantern-bearer led the way. The donkey-driver's lamp flickered as he drove through the gates. Once again, a procession wound along the narrow streets of Manatas to the waterfront.

Halvar stopped to gaze down Pearl Street, where lights shone in the tiny windows of the three houses. The Danic house was decorated with a bough of mixed holly and pine hung over the front door. The Bretain house had a lantern set in the window, visible from the street..

The center house, occupied by Milord and Milady Summersby, was the only one with no outside decorations. However, it was definitely inhabited. There was a glimmer of light in the front window. A shrill voice could be heard berating someone within.

Halvar grinned. Franchen was not one of his languages, but he knew invective when he heard it. Words like *fool*…*stupid*…

There was a murmured response he couldn't make out, but he caught the gist of what Milady was saying.

"I won't stay here in this miserable hovel! There's no one to talk to now that Franz is gone."

More unheard response.

"He didn't mean any harm, he just paid me a few compliments. He should have stayed here, with us, but no, he had to go off to his whore, and he left me in this sty! I could have killed him myself!"

Flores cocked an eyebrow at Halvar.

"Does she know she can be overheard?"

"I don't think she cares," Halvar replied. "She's got a temper, that one."

"Did Milord do it?"

Halvar frowned. "I'm not sure. He's got that man of his, Edgar, who'll swear that he was in the house all night. He's not Andalusian, so we can't arrest him until we get firm proof of his guilt. As far as I can tell, he had every reason to keep Girard alive, at least until they got to Bella Mara. "

"What about the other one, the soldier?"

"I'll question him tonight, at the taberna. He knows more than he's telling about Girard. You and your men have to find Ibo, fast, but I fear it's too late."

"And if it is?"

"Even the dead can speak, if you know the questions to ask," Halvar said, quoting Old Sergeant Olaf.

The leading guardsman had reached the plaza and the Mermaid Taberna.

"I'm going to have a little chat with my old comrade Devallon," Halvar told Flores. "Keep looking until you find Ibo."

He headed for the warmth and conviviality of his new lodgings, leaving Flores to fume in the chill of an early winter evening in Manatas.

132

Chapter 17

THE MERMAID TABERNA WAS DOING GOOD business for a slow time of year. The large central room was not as full as it would have been during a feria, when merchants and seamen met to bargain over cargoes, but several Andalusians sat at the low tables ranged along one wall, puffing on water-pipes, while Oropans perched on stools at higher tables, smoking clay pipes.

Two Halfling lads ran between the kitchen and the central room carrying mugs of mokka and tankards of ale, as well as platters of meat and bowls of rich soup. The air was redolent with the odors of roasting meats and spicy sauces, tabac, ale and mokka.

Hannes Zilberstam stumped from one table to another, chuffing with his usual customers, greeting everyone with "Good Yule" or "May Chesu bless you at his Nativity" and even "May your fast be righteous in the eyes of Ilha and his Prophet." Halvar's stomach rumbled, reminding him he hadn't ingested anything but mokka since his break-the-fast many hours ago.

"Hola! Danske! Sit with us!" Baltasar beckoned Halvar over to one of the tables whose top was decorated with the inlaid board used for the game the Bretains called backgammon and everyone else just called tables.

"Not tonight." Halvar scanned the room for a certain face, and found it in his favorite spot, the table nearest the stairs leading to his private quarters. "I have a guest. An old companion from Oropa, new to Manatas."

"Bring him over, if he's good at tables," Lukas called as Halvar made his way through the taberna to where Devallon had made himself at home.

Devallon's long legs protruded into the narrow space between the table and the stairs. He had opened his jacket to reveal a linen shirt, which, in turn, was loosened to revealed a tuft of chest hair at the collar. He had a bowl of soup in front of him and a tankard of ale in his hand.

"God be with ye, Devallon," Halvar said in Erse. "Got away from Milord and Milady, did you?"

"He's dealing with the sailors at Maison Rouge, she's in a fit of the sulks, and I'm not necessary for either of those. What a pair!" Devallon said. "Your host has made me welcome enough." He lifted the tankard in a toast.

Halvar noted the food on the table.

"I see you've sampled our local cuisine. How do you like it?"

"What's in this stuff?" Devallon stirred the bowl with a wooden spoon and ignored the helping of fresh green sallet and slice of crusty bread that accompanied the savory stew, provided at no extra cost by the usually thrifty Fru Marta in honor of the season.

"Fowl, usually," Halvar said. He gestured to one Halfling server. "I'll have my usual."

The lad dashed off towards the kitchen.

"Foul it is," Devallon grumbled. "No pork, I suppose?"

"Not in Islim country," Halvar said. He looked up as the Halfling deposited a clay mug and a bowl before him. "Aha! Mokka! And good soup, very filling." He sniffed eagerly. "I think Fru Marta's baked some of her fruit pastries special for the feast days."

Devallon took another bite of the thick soup.

"Not too bad, if you don't mind getting your tongue burned off halfway to your stomach," he decided.

Halvar accepted his portion and spooned it up eagerly.

"Better than field rations, Musket-man. I've eaten worse in my time. So have you."

"Not willingly," Devallon said. "So, Pikeman, how do you come to be Capitán in Manatas?"

"Long story or short?"

"I'm not going anywhere." Devallon took another spoonful of soup. "Last I saw of the Danes was Pisa. What happened at Pisa?"

"You would have known if you'd looked behind you when you were running as fast as you could to get away from the battle. Lovis used the cannons, and we got cut to pieces. The Pisans surrendered. What else could they do?"

"They could have given in when Lovis's troops arrived instead of trying to fight him. Our lot saw reason and signed on with the companies joining the troops in Hispania. Only fools like the Danes would try to beat Lovis."

"When you buy the Danes, the Danes stay bought," Halvar stated. "We were paid, we stayed. And died well, no wounds in the back. I lost most of my friends on that field, and nearly lost my left arm as well."

"It's still there," Devallon pointed out.

"Thanks to a surgeon and a very loud lady, who insisted on hauling any of the wounded who still had breath off to the medical tents."

"And so, you lived. How did you wind up in Al-Andalus?

"I got put on the wrong cart," Halvar said. "One was supposed to take the wounded back to Pisa to be sent back where they came from, the other to the ship bound for Al-Andalus. I got into the lot for Al-Andalus and wound up in the care of the Sisters of Fatima in Corduva. Quite a formidable set of ladies they are, too. We have one of their Houses of the Green Crescent here in Manatas. If you're ever wounded, make sure you go there to be cured. They'll take care of you until you can walk on your own."

"And then?"

Halvar grinned under his mustache.

"You're on your own. They give you a clean set of clothes and a dinar, and that's that."

"Which left you…?"

"In Corduva, with no money, not knowing much Arabi. I went to spend my last dinar in the nearest taberna, which happened to be where the students at the madrassa liked to revel. There was a quarrel, someone drew a knife on a young fellow, I thought I'd stop the fight.

"Turned out the young fellow was Don Felipe, the old calif's grandson. Next thing I knew, I had the post of personal bodyguard and watchdog, following the lad around Corduva."

"Sounds like something out of those kitchen-tales my granny used to tell."

"I think the Three Old Women were looking out for me," Halvar said, and meant it. "And when Don Felipe rose to be calif in his own good time, he kept me on as his Hireling, sent me here and there, to take care of this and that.

"And so, I came to Manatas on such an errand, but things got, um, complicated. At the end of the Fall Feria, I was appointed capitán of the Town Guards. And that's my story. What about you, Devallon? Before I left Al-Andalus—"

"Hispania, now," Devallon corrected him.

"Al-Andalus," Halvar repeated stubbornly, "there was some talk of Lovis the Younger reorganizing his forces, putting all the free companies under one commander."

Devallon sighed mightily.

"That he did. Once Hispania was settled, he disbanded everyone. No more free companies, each under its own commander, each taking its own commissions. Only one army—his. We had two choices—join the Franchen Army, or find other employment."

"Sounds like a good thing, having only one army. At least you'd get paid," Halvar said. "Free companies don't, sometimes. Of course, being a pikeman, it wasn't for me to argue. Besides, my first three years' pay went to my Thane, to repay my father's debt. All I got was my food and the companionship of the other Danes."

"And the chance of being blown to bits by those damned cannons," Devallon said, taking a pull at his tankard. "What is this stuff?"

"Ale," Halvar told him after a sniff. "Not bad, for Bretain-brewed. I stick to mokka. "

"No wine?" Devallon stared into the tankard.

"Not allowed in Manats, by order of Mullah Abadul. Seems the Prophet didn't approve of wine. Nothing said against ale, of course," he added, with a wink. "Or you can go to the Gardens of Paradise in Green Village. They've got a special dispensation to serve alcohol. If you want to get totally unconscious, there's a cider that will lay you out flat. It sneaks up on you, tastes like fruit juice, until you try to stand and can't find your footing."

He recalled his first night at the Gardens of Paradise, when he had been rendered insensible by the combination of cider, hemp, and a blow to the back of his head.

"So, tell me, ex-Musket-man, what did you decide to do? You had three friends, as I remember it."

Devallon sighed mightily and took another pull of ale.

"I had friends, but no more. The Toff decided to go back to his estate. The Prig made good on his vow to become a prester. The Lad took the offer of an army commission, and for all I know, he's still fighting in Hispania.

"As for me, I have no estate, don't want to be a prester, and the idea of taking orders from the likes of the Lad didn't sit well. So, I looked about for something else."

"And found Milord Summersby?"

"Not in Franchenland. What I found was a berth on the ship carrying the King's Daughters to Kibbick."

"Those women Lovis the Younger was sending to take the place of the Local wives?" Halvar's grin widened. "That must have been an interesting voyage."

"If you like dealing with two dozen seasick females." Devallon grimaced. "A few of them were able to take care of the rest. Once they found their sea legs, they were more trouble than you'd think possible. My job was to keep the sailors off the girls. Old Dame Brigitte was supposed to keep the girls off the sailors, but she was one of the seasick ones. I don't know which of us had the worse time of it."

"What about Girard?" Halvar asked, beckoning to the serving-lad for refills. "I hear he was a ladies' man. Was he, um, sampling the wares?"

"That he did not." Devallon accepted a fresh tankard with a nod and a smirk. "He knew better than that! Oh, he chatted a few of them up, but no more than that. Not that they didn't try to attract his notice, especially not little Charlotte, but Girard wouldn't play her games. She just had to wait until we got to Kibbick."

"Charlotte?"

"Milady Summersby," Devallon said. "But not on the ship. As I said, that had to wait until Kibbick."

"Where they met their future husbands," Halvar said. "How was that arranged?"

"The girls were auctioned off. Each one came with a dowry of ten silver imperials, which bought nothing in Kibbick, because there was nothing to buy, and a land grant, which was worth a good deal more.

"Of course, the land has to be cleared, but once it is, there's the deed to keep it in perpetuity for the girl's husband and any of her offspring. So, the farmers and soldiers and the trappers bid, and the one with the most beaver pelts won the prize."

"And Summersby?"

"Ah, Summersby. He caught Charlotte's eye and bid in gold for her, and won her silver and her land. He took one look at the land and decided to trade with one of the officers at the fort who had a parcel coming to him in Powhatan—what's now Terra Mara. The officer took Milady's land grant, Summersby got the papers that proved he was heir to the grant in Terra Mara, near this new town, BelMar, and hired Girard to take him there.

"Dame Brigitte stuck with Charlotte, and I presented myself to him as an able fighter who knew both Erse and Arabi as well as Franchen. So, now you know my story."

Devallon leaned back against the wall and scrabbled in his jacket pocket. He pulled out a small clay pipe and a leather pouch.

"Tabac?" He offered it to Halvar.

"Never took to it."

"Your loss." Devallon filled his pipe and looked around for a straw to light it with. The Halfling server was there with a long sliver of wood, smoking at one end. Devallon looked up, nodded, and lit his pipe.

"Ah!" He took a long drag. "The only good thing that ever came out of this misbegotten Nova Mundum. Tabac!"

Halvar's nose wrinkled at the aroma. Tabac might be soothing to some, but he had never cared for the smell of burnt leaves that seemed to hang over those who indulged.

"You spent more time with Girard than anyone I've met, except for his crew," he said. "Two Franchen men on a ship full of women and sailors. A captain can't talk to the sailors, and the mate was a drunkard. What did you make of Girard?"

Devallon took a thoughtful puff at his pipe.

"Canny," he pronounced. "Clever, with an eye to the main chance, as the merchants put it. He owned his ship, had the right to take a part of the cargo and sell it at his own profit. And profit was what he cared about."

"He carried passengers, too," Halvar pointed out.

"That's what I mean," Devallon said. "Most captains won't take passengers, hate to have the trouble. I heard from the mate, Michel Primero, about the Afrikans he carried from Savana Port in the spring, how they demanded special food, got sick, there were problems about the women on board, the big leader kept trying to give orders, the youngster had to know everything about everything—just a nuisance.

"But Girard made them pay well for the voyage, and he took a healthy sum for transporting those women, too. In silver imperials, no less!"

"He must have spent of it some refurbishing his ship. I saw those quarters for quality folk—they looked reasonably comfortable. Better than what I got on the dhow coming over. And the large cabin, for the lesser folk? Not too bad, considering. I suppose they put down pallets for sleeping and cleared them away during the day."

Devallon nodded. "Quality cabins, to be sure. On the voyage out to Kibbick, I got one to share with an officer from Franchenland. The other went to Dame Brigitte, who was supposed to arrange the marriages when they got to Kibbick."

"With an auction?"

"My opinion?" Devallon's smirk grew broader. "If there had been a proper brothel already set up in Kibbick, those girls would never have met the prester. But the governor was there to take charge, and he had the pick of the lot, and confiscated the proceeds from the auction. Said it was 'For the betterment of the colony.' Ha!"

He laughed without real humor.

"And that left Dame Brigitte with no girls, and no way back to Franchenland. So, when Charlotte nailed

141

Henry Summersby, she insisted on going along with her."

"She didn't strike me as the lady's-maid type," Halvar commented. "Quite a mouth on her, that one. Was she sick once she got away from Kibbick?"

"That she was, but Charlotte was on deck any time the sea was calm."

"With Girard in attendance?"

Devallon blew a cloud of smoke.

"She was working it between them," he said, with a wink. "She'd already got Henry, but she's the sort wants every man in sight to be at her feet. Even tried it on me, during the voyage out to Kibbick.

"Mind you, I knew I had no real chance, so I flirted, but no more. As for Girard…he had other fish to fry. Besides, he liked big, boozy Bretains, like Long Liz, not dainty Franchen with expensive tastes."

Halvar digested this information with another sip of mokka.

"It must have been an interesting voyage south from Kibbick" he mused. "Only the four of you, three Franchen to one Bretain. Not counting the crew, that is."

Their discourse was interrupted by Hannes stamping into the center of the room, where the tables had been cleared to make a space.

"I crave your attention, my friends! We have a most special treat for you tonight, in celebration of Nativity and Yule and the end of Fasting Month!"

There was a sudden flourish of drumming and a blast of a trumpet. Halvar winced as he saw an all-too-familiar figure, clad in striped trews, checked jacket, and wide-brimmed hat decorated with a gobbler's feathers. He knew what was coming next.

"You might want to get back to the Summersby household," he murmured to Devallon. "We have some entertainment coming. Our genial host has spent a few pennies to bring Manatas's chief storyteller and comic singer to the Mermaid Taberna."

Hannes announced, "Friends, I give you...Willem of Cos!"

The well-known performer took his place in the center of the room. He bowed, flourishing his hat at Halvar and Devallon.

"Here it comes," Halvar muttered. He prepared himself for yet another rendition of the ballad that had sealed his reputation in Manatas as the Man Who was Sprayed by the Sekonk.

He was pleasantly surprised when Willem instead announced, "A song for the season!" and began an old ditty in Erse, caroling the arrival of the Redeemer, as told in the Holy Books.

"At least he's not doing 'The Stranger and the Sekonk,'" Halvar muttered into his mokka.

Willem's repertoire was larger than Halvar had thought. He went on to tell some clever stories in Arabi about the Wise Hodja, then led another song with a joyous chorus of "Fa-la-la."

Devallon rose then, unsteady on his feet.

"Do you know this one?" He started to sing, in a melodious baritone:

> Oh, to be in Nova Mundum,
> If you take ship, all can come,
> Why remain in Old Oropa,
> Living under Lovis' thumb.

> In Nova, Nova Mundum,
> Nova, Nova Mundum,
> Nova Nova Nova Nova
> Nova Nova Mundum.

The rollicking tune reminded Halvar of one of the dances he'd learned as a boy in the Dane-March.

Devallon went on:

> In Nova Mundum land is free,
> Plant your cabbage, wheat and
> > oats,
> Find a Local girl to marry,

"Till her brothers cut your throats!" Willem shot back.

There was a general roar of laughter at this, and everyone joined in the chorus, pounding on the tables to keep the rhythm.

Now it was Willem's turn:

> You can settle in West Caster,
> Hunt for furs, cast nets for fish.

Baltasar cut in with a retort:

> Better come here to Manatas,
> Worship any god you wish.

Devallon and Baltasar started prancing among the tables, leading the men in a raucous dance. Willem's trumpeter and drummer picked up the tempo.

> And if you want to be a king,
> To Nova Mundum you must go,
> Any lout in Old Oropa
> Lives like a lord in a year or so!

Devallon collapsed back onto the bench after the last chorus, gasping and laughing at the same time. Hannes hustled over with another tankard of ale.

"Good song, friend! You may stay as long as you like—everyone's buying more mokka and ale to settle their thirst."

Halvar sighed. "I hate to cut this short, Devallon, but I've got my business to attend to, and you've got Milord's. Better get back to their house. Milady seems to be out of temper, perhaps you can soothe her."

"Oh, she's finished with me," Devallon said, with a wry twist of his lips. "Once we landed in Kibbick, she had no time for a mere soldier. She was after larger game.

"As for that house, it's small for five. Milord, Milady, Edgar, Brigitte, they got the upstairs beds. Me? I slept on the table in the front room. I don't suppose there's a bed in a room here, landlord?

"According to Girard, there are sleeping-rooms upstairs in this place. He said that when he was here last spring, there was some fellow who had taken them, but he spent his time in some place called Green Village and wouldn't be put out if we took them temporarily."

"Leon di Vicenza is now in Green Village Fratery, and those rooms are my quarters," Halvar said firmly. "*Private* quarters." After all those years of barracks and shared bedrooms, he valued the opportunity to be alone in his own bed.

Devallon sighed deeply. "It's a cold night," he said plaintively. "And you wouldn't wish an old friend to be forced to listen to that shrew, would you?"

"You're no friend of mine," Halvar said. "And there's but one bed, and it's mine. Don't take offense, Devallon, but I'm getting used to sleeping without company snoring in my ear. Why don't you go to La Maison Rouge? I'm sure they'd have a bed for you there."

"And four others to fill it," Devallon sneered. "I should hope I'm a cut above that!"

Hannes looked from one old soldier to the other.

"There are two rooms," he reminded Halvar. "If I put a pallet on the floor of the sitting room, Heer De-

145

vallon can make himself comfortable there. And I will only charge him five purple wumpum, which will come off *your* bill, Capitán."

Halvar hesitated. Why couldn't he just tell the old musket-man to get back to his milord? The truth was, he wouldn't subject a dog to the virago who called herself Milady Summersby.

"I'll take the pallet," Devallon said.

"I'll have the lad take it up," Hannes promised him.

They were interrupted by Zoltan and Fergus, both looking thoroughly unhappy as they crossed to where Halvar sat.

"Capitán! Tenente Flores wants you right now," Fergus told him.

"You've found Ibo?" Halvar looked from one man to the other.

"That we have," Zoltan said. "He's in the latrine."

"And he's dead," Fergus added.

"I thought he might be." Halvar got up with a sigh. "Stay here, Devallon, this doesn't concern you. Hannes, why don't you let my friend have some of your fine cider? The special jug from West Caster?"

Hannes bowed and smirked.

"Of course, landsman! I'll see Heer Devallon gets the best."

Devallon leaned back against the wall and surveyed the room.

"It's right chilly tonight," he observed. "And black as the Pit of Hades. I wish you the joy of your job, Capitán. I'll be here when you get back."

Halvar gritted his teeth as he fastened his coat against the evening chill and joined the squad at the door. Whatever they had found would not be pleasant to look at.

Chapter 18

HALVAR FOLLOWED THE TWO GUARDSMEN, who held lanterns on poles, around the taberna to the reeking path that led to the latrine, where Flores waited for him with Zoltan and Fergus.

"How did you come to find him?" Halvar asked.

"It wasn't exactly us," Zoltan said, with a look of chagrin. "It was these fellows." He nodded to three men standing next to the shack that gave those who needed it some privacy.

"We was coming off our stand," the tallest, an Afrikan, said, in hesitant Arabi. "We fish, sell to women."

"We go to bog before we go home," the second man, whose caftan and twisted turban proclaimed his Andalusian ancestry, said.

"And we see...him!" The third fisherman, a halfling in a deerskin hunting shirt and Andalusian trousers gasped, still shocked at the ghastly sight.

Halvar looked into the privy. At first glance, it was empty. When he stepped in and turned as if to to sit on the wooden seat that covered the bucket for the daily offerings, he came face-to-face with the stiffened corpse, jammed into the corner behind the opened door.

"Get him out!" he ordered, suppressing the urge to scream. It was now obvious why no one had found the unfortunate Ibo until now. A superficial glance inside the privy would not have revealed his body; only someone actually using the station would have seen him, and who would use the place in such weather?

No one moved.

"What are you waiting for?" Halvar stepped back onto the path.

"Bad juju to touch the dead," the Afrikan fisherman mumbled.

"Against the Prophet's word," said the Andalusian

"Not good," the halfling agreed. "His ghost might come back."

"His ghost will haunt whoever did this to him," Halvar asserted. "You didn't do it, so you should be safe."

A donkey pulling a cart from the Rabat trotted down the path, carrying Dr. Moise and Selim.

"You do find interesting things at the worst possible times," the lanky Afrikan complained. "I was just sitting down to an end-of-fast meal when I heard you'd found another body."

"And I knew you'd want me to be here to take notes," Selim added, glaring defiantly at Halvar. "Is it Ibo?"

"It's an Afrikan," Halvar said. "I suppose we'll have to wait until morning to send for the Scavengers to identify him."

"No, you won't." Selim waved at a line of torches heading their way, carried by a procession of ragged men, all armed with large clubs or knives. "It looks like they've gotten the word already."

The Scavengers blocked the path back to the Rabat. Rachev came forward, with Osman behind him.

"We've come for Ibo!" he announced.

"You haven't wasted any time," Halvar said, looking over the assembled ragamuffins. "How did you find out so hast?"

Rachev smirked. "We have our sources. Our lads and gals keep their eyes open. We have a girl posted at the gate of the Rabat. As soon as she saw Tenente Flores heading here, she ran and got me."

"So, here you are, and it will do you no good. This body goes to the Rabat for examination."

"So your doctor can cut him to pieces? Never! We want him for proper burial." Rachev took another step forward, holding his bludgeon in the hand that still had all its fingers.

"All victims of unnatural deaths are to be examined by our doctor," Flores recited. "It's what our Excellent Sultan ordered, and that's what we'll do. Isn't that right, Capitán?"

He looked to Halvar for approval.

"It goes against the Prophet's writings," Osman quavered from behind his larger friend. "And it doesn't matter, anyway. We already know who did this. It was the Franchen soldier."

"What is your proof?" Halvar demanded. "If one of those wide-eyed youngsters saw the murder, let him come forward and give evidence, and we'll arrest the Franchen. If not, then the matter rests until we have proof. So says Sharia."

"They may be right, Capitán," Flores suggested. "The Franchen carries a sword and a dagger—that poniard thing."

"So do a number of others," Halvar said. "And he uses tabac. But that's not enough to convince me he's the killer."

"You're protecting him because he's Oropan, like you," Rachev sneered. "We're going to take our brother for burial, and then we'll get that Franchen!"

He moved forward, hefting his club.

"Not on my watch," Halvar fumed. He waved to the guardsmen, not taking his eyes off Rachev. "Town Guard, to your posts! Line up like I showed you. We can't let them take the body before we've had it examined."

Flores's squad lined up across the path, halberds ready. Flores glanced nervously at Halvar.

"Why not just let him take the Franchen soldier and be done with it?"

"If we give in to them, they'll think they run Manatas," Halvar said.

"We do!" Rachev snarled. He took another step forward. "Do you think you know Manatas, Danske? You don't know shit!"

"I know what I've sworn to do," Halvar retorted. "Don Felipe himself said it. 'Keep Manatas safe,' he told me, and I'll do it. You lift a hand to my men, and we'll arrest you as rioters. That's treason against our most noble calif, Don Felipe, may he live long. You don't want that, do you?"

Rachev hesitated for a moment. Then he roared, "Get them!"

The Scavengers surged forward. Halvar grabbed one of the halberds and thrust it out to push them back up the hill. The lantern-bearers tried to get out of the way as the two groups struggled on the slippery stones of the path.

Crazy shadows played against the walls of the taberna and the latrines as guardsmen thrust the axe-heads of the halberds at the ragged beggars, who dodged and slashed out with bludgeons and knives. A shriek meant that something had connected, a thump and a curse meant a club had missed.

"This won't do!" Halvar tried to rally his troops. "Crosswise, you dolts! Push them back!"

He held the halberd across his body, turning the blade so the flat side faced the mob. Flores shoved his men into position, struggling to keep his footing on the path that was rapidly turning into icy mud.

Halvar slid into one wall, staggered and nearly fell. He felt a hand under his elbow, righted himself, and pushed forward. His boots were covered with muck, and he felt foul dampness oozing onto the cuffs of his breeches.

Slowly, Halvar's guardsmen pushed the Scavengers back up the hill to Pearl Street, where there were lanterns in front of the three houses, as per the orders of the sultan. Another lantern hung from a pole in front of the henhouse, and a third swung next to the door of the mokka-shop on the Broad Way.

The mob aroused the hens and geese who had settled for the night around the henhouse and in the vegetable plot. The hens set up a squawking, the rooster crowed his displeasure at the intruders. The geese honked loudly and flapped their wings at the mere men who dared disturb their nesting site.

Doors popped open. A large Dane emerged from one house carrying a hefty club; a man in Bretain trews and patterned woolen shirt came from the farthest house, armed with a cumbersome but impressive blunderbuss.

"What's going on?" the Danic householder demanded.

"Nothing to worry about, good folk," Halvar assured them, grandly waving at the guardsmen. "You

151

will hear all about it from the news-crier tomorrow. The body of a Scavenger was found in the latrine at the end of the path. We are taking the poor fellow to the Rabat so that we can find out who did this dreadful thing. Once we have finished, we will turn him over to his friends for proper Islim burial."

"Scavenger?" The Dane spat his disdain. "Good riddance, then."

"Not just any Scavenger," Rachev said. "It was Ibo the Afrikan, who cleans the jakes. Think of that when you have to deal with your own filth!"

"Ibo?" The Bretain lowered his firearm "That's ridiculous. Who'd kill poor old Ibo?"

"That's what we're going to find out," Halvar assured him. "Go back to your homes, good folk. The town of Manatas is being served well." He turned to the mob. "These men are leaving... Now!"

Halvar poked Rachev with the point of the halberd. The Scavenger had managed to avoid being slashed, but Osman had not been so lucky.

"I've been cut," Osman whined, clutching his arm where someone's blade had ripped into it.

"Get to the House of the Green Crescent," Flores jeered. "They'll look after anyone."

"Dr. Moise, I think you can take this poor fellow to the Rabat," Halvar said.

The guardsmen moved the Scavengers aside, and the donkey cart went through. Selim rode triumphantly next to the doctor, grinning happily.

What now? Halvar wondered. He knew he should accompany Dr. Moise and the cart back to the Rabat, but to what purpose? Nothing could be done until daylight, and it had been a very long day. Two fights, two murders, and he still didn't know who had done the ghastly deeds.

True, Devallon *was* the most likely suspect, but why would the Franchen kill the one man who could get him out of the one place in Nova Mundum where he least desired to be? Milord Summersby was vouched for by his wife and servants, and the same reasoning held for him. He wanted to go to Bella Mara, so why kill the navigator who could get him there?

A good night's sleep will help, Halvar decided.

He watched tiny points of light fade as the lanterns and torches were carried up the hill and disappeared into the darkness of the early winter night. The sky was covered in clouds—no moonlight or starlight to ease the gloom. There was just enough lantern light for him to make his way down the path, back to the comfort and warmth of the Mermaid Taberna.

As he headed towards his quarters, Halvar glanced at the middle house in the row on Pearl Street. Of all the buildings, this was the only one whose door had remained shut.

Chapter 19

AS HALVAR STARTED UP THE OUTSIDE STAIR
that led to his private quarters, Hannes Zilberstam
popped out of the pantry door under the staircase.

"Finished with the body?" he asked.

"For now," Halvar replied. He jerked his head upward. "What about my friend?"

"The musket-man? He's down for the night. That
cider was more than he's used to." Hannes chuckled.
"I had my lad put him to bed upstairs.

"But there's another lot in there asking for you. A
gang of Franchen sailors, and a Bretain Milord with
them."

"What do they want with me?" Hannes wondered
aloud as he followed Hannes through the taberna
kitchens.

Fru Marta clucked over the state of his clothes.

"Faugh! You smell worse than a sekonk!"

"Not my fault!" Halvar protested, as the woman pulled his coat off. "The Scavengers attacked us as we were taking the body of Ibo the Afrikan to the Rabat."

"Ibo?"

"Found in the jakes," Halvar explained as Fru Marta helped him into the coat she had cleaned earlier that day "What's this about Franchen sailors?"

Hannes ushered him into the main room, which was now empty of customers. Once the night prayers were done, and the bells in the Kristo chapel rang for the final benediction, folk in Manatas preferred to seek their lodgings while the lanterns still burned rather than grope their way in the dark. Only the two gamblers, Baltasar and Lukas, remained lounging on the bench behind their backgammon table with the boy Jeannot seated between them.

Standing before them were Michel Primero and two of his men. Milord Summersby sat at a nearby table, moodily contemplating a mug of something that steamed and smelled of fruit and spices.

"A Bretain specialty—mulled cider," Hannes explained, handing a similar mug to Halvar. "Not the special jug, the sweet one. Supposed to be good as a before-bed drink, to put one in a proper mood for sleep."

"With that wife of his, he likely needs it," Halvar muttered. He took a sip and nodded. "Tasty!"

"Expensive, too," Hannes said. "Those spices don't come cheap. But he's footing the bill, so drink up, landsman." He clapped his hands for attention. "My good friends, Capitán Don Alvaro Dánico has arrived. He will sort out your complaints." He added, "We will speak in Erse so that Milord Summersby, who has hired these men, will understand what we say."

Halvar was confused.

"What has this to do with me? I'm not in charge of the waterfront—that's for the sultan and the calif's tally-men. They're in charge of the books, not me. Go talk to them."

"You have the ear of Sultan Petrus," Michel said. "You can explain to him that we must put our crewmen on board the *Belle Fleur* at first light. She can't be allowed to stay unattended during the coming storm."

"You think there will be a storm?" Halvar countered. "I haven't seen a flake of snow yet."

"The wind is already picking up," Michel pointed out. "The stars are covered with cloud. The tide is coming in, hard and fast. There will be snow tomorrow, I can smell it. If, as Jeannot says, you killed Bayard and the others, then there is no one to set the sails and point the ship out of the wind. We must be allowed to go back to her."

"I'm not stopping you," Halvar said. "Your captain sailed into the harbor with no by-your-leave, and he never got you registered, so as far as the tally-man is concerned, you were never here."

"Exactly what I said," Summersby interjected from his seat at the table. "But these fellows won't go unless they are assured no one will follow them."

"You mean Locals in canoes?" Halvar shrugged. "Those are the watchmen, looking for raiders coming in, not sailing ships going out. Firebrand's seen what you've got, which is an empty ship. If you want to take it away, I won't stop you, and neither will they. But Milord and Milady stay here, with their servants."

"What about the boy?" Michel looked fiercely at Baltasar. Lukas laid a hand on Jeannot's shoulder.

"If Jeannot doesn't want to come with you, he is welcome to stay with us," Lukas said, glaring at Michel.

"He's apprenticed to Captain Girard, he sails with us," Michel shot back.

"He's been mistreated. We saw the bruises from the beatings," Baltasar said.

"He's got to learn, same as the rest of us," Michel insisted.

"That's not the way to teach anyone anything."

Halvar decided to put an end to the argument.

"Jeannot, it's up to you. Do you want to go back to the ship, or stay here with these two? You know what's waiting for you on the ship, you don't know what these two will do."

Jeannot shrank back against Baltasar's shoulder.

"I stay here," he decided.

"So, that's that," Halvar stated. "Milord, if there's a storm brewing, you should get to your own house."

"A good thought," Hannes agreed. "I heard the chapel bell signaling the end of night prayers. All good souls should be indoors. It's time for this place to close."

Halvar peeked out the door. There was no glimmer of moon or starlight. The only sound was the lapping of waves against the piers.

"Hannes, can you spare one of your lads to light Milord up the path to his house?"

"Oh, Edgar can do that. He's waiting at the door with the lantern." Summersby heaved up and staggered to the door, where his faithful servant wrapped him in a cloak.

"Our lodging is up the path toward Broad Way," Baltasar said, wrapping himself in a heavy fox-fur trimmed cloak. "If you don't mind, Milord, we'll walk with you, save our host from having to send one of his lads out with us. Jeannot, one more time—there's a bed for you with us, if you want to take it."

"With who else in it?" sneered Michel. "Lad, you can still come with us to Maison Rouge. You're listed as ship's boy, you're entitled to a wage."

Jeannot looked from Baltasar to Michel.

"No beatings?"

157

Michel cleared his throat.

"Can't promise that."

"Then I stay with Baltasar." Jeannot followed the two gamblers to the door.

"He'll be back with us on the ship tomorrow," Michel promised his men. He turned back to Halvar. "With your permission, Capitán, we'll row out to the ship tomorrow as soon as the tide turns. and we'll take Captain Girard with us, when your doctor lets us have his body. We'll give him back to the sea once we get far out enough he won't wash up on shore."

"That's for Dr. Moise to decide," Halvar said. "Once he's made his examination, the body's no use to him. Whether it goes to the burying ground here on Manatas or the sea, that's your concern, not mine." He yawned mightily. It had been a long day. "Have you found a navigator?"

Milord called out from the doorway, "Edgar has studied mathematics, and he watched the captain. I can read a chart as well as anyone. Michel Primero can steer. Among us, we should be able to get to BelMar in a week or two."

Michel sketched a bow.

"As you say, Milord." He jerked his head at the Halfling server. "Lad, you can light us to La Maison Rouge, and there's a penny for you if you don't betray us to robbers."

"I take wumpum only," the Halfling said with injured dignity.

The two groups marched out, leaving Halvar alone with Hannes.

"What about the musket-man?"

"Upstairs, like I said. Here's your candle. Sleep well, landsman."

Halvar made his way up the inside stair. Each step reminded him he'd had a very active day. Two fights in twenty-four hours? At least no one had been after him in particular, for a change.

The candle lit the sitting-room, where a straw-stuffed mattress had been laid out on the floor next to the square table with its two stools. Halvar's heart sank as he realized there was no one on the pallet. He checked the inner room. Sure enough, Devallon had commandeered the huge bed, where he lay, sprawled across the huge piece of furniture, snoring heartily.

The old soldier's gear lay in a tumbled pile on the floor next to the bed. Halvar automatically sorted it out—coat, shabby, but serviceable, cut in the style used by the free companies ten years before; breeches wide enough to fit easily, but tight enough to show off a good leg; belt and sword. He picked up Devallon's boots and checked their soles. No muck, but the ground had been hard with frost.

Then, he held the candle closer to the sword's hilt and cursed softly. He knew that symbol etched on the hilt.

Odd, he thought. Devallon had a sword, but where was his poniard—the long thin knife that matched the sword? Most Franchen swordsmen carried both. No pistoia, either, although someone had mentioned that the bodyguard carried one.

Halvar could hear Old Sergeant Olaf's voice in his head: *Everything is important, even what isn't there.* He'd have to find that poniard.

But now not. In the morning, he'd have another word or two with his unwanted guest.

He glumly considered his options. There was room enough for him to ease onto that big bed. Leon *had* had it constructed to hold two men, after all.

But Halvar thought of what that fleur-de-lys meant, and where he had last seen it. A pallet on the floor was preferable to sleeping with a murderer.

159

Thor's Hammer! He's out of here by morning, Halvar thought as he took off his fouled boots and his fresh-ly-cleaned coat. He clutched his amulet and recited his final prayer: *May the Redeemer and Mother Mara and the god Thor keep me safe until morning.*

He eased down onto the pallet. His last thought before sleep claimed him was *If Milord was at Maison Rouge with those sailors, and Devallon was here, who was Milady yelling at?*

Chapter 20

HALVAR WAS SHOCKED AWAKE BY A BLAST OF cold air. He rolled off the pallet, stiff and achy, to find a pair of boots looming over him. Hands heaved him to his feet. It was Flores his face a mask of chagrin.

"Bad news, Capitán," he stated. "We've found another one."

"Another what?"

Halvar ran a hand through his hair and scratched the stubble on his chin. He wanted the latrine, the *hammam* and a barber, and mokka, not necessarily in that order.

"Body," Flores said, handing him his clothes.

Halvar hauled his breeches on over his braies and shrugged into his coat. He looked for his two caps. Both had served well to protect his head from blows. He felt naked without them.

"Whose body"

"Long Liz."

That got Halvar's attention.

"What? When?" He fastened the toggles on the coat and finished this sketchy toilette by buckling his belt over the coat so that his dagger, with the amber in the hilt, was close to hand.

He suddenly remembered his unwanted roommate.

"Devallon…" he began, as he stepped over to the curtain that separated sleeping from sitting quarters.

The bed was empty. Devallon was gone.

Halvar clutched his amulet and muttered his morning plea to the Redeemer and Mother Mara and Thor for help. It looked as if he would need it.

"It was Zoltan found her," Flores explained as he followed Halvar down the outside stairs. "He sent one of Prester Nicodemus's lads to the Rabat with the word. I sent for Eva Hakim—it's she who takes care of women's bodies, after all; but Dr. Moise insisted on coming with the cart, and I couldn't stop young Selim from joining him."

Halvar strode across the plaza and northward on Maiden Lane. Zoltan and Fergus were standing in front of Liz's shack, trying to hold back several women in various states of undress, regardless of the chilly wind whistling across the bay.

"You did the right thing. Good work, Tenente Flores." Halvar nodded to the donkey driver and waved a sketchy salaam to Dr. Moise and Selim.

"You got here in good time," he commented.

"We have to find out who is doing this!" Selim exclaimed. "Three deaths in a day!"

The waiting women echoed her sentiments, loudly, in several languages. A shout interrupted the babble.

"Make way for Eva Hakim!" Fergus called from the north end of Maiden Lane.

The tall female physician bustled forward, a short Local woman trotting after her. Both carried baskets, presumably containing the tools of the medical profession.

Dr, Moise greeted his colleague.

"*Salaam aleikum*, Eva Hakim. I'm sorry to tell you, this is no sight for a woman."

"I have seen worse, I assure you," Eva Hakim said. "It is not right that a man should examine a woman's body."

"Many men have examined this woman's body," Flores said with a coarse laugh.

"Let me pass, Guardsman Flores!" She thrust him aside.

Halvar followed her into the room and gasped.

The crib, small though it was, had been neatly arranged when he was there before. Now, it looked as if someone had gone bear-shirt in it. The small chest at the foot of the bed was overturned, its contents spilled on the floor. The little box with Liz's store of cheap ornaments had been thrown on top of it. The very pillows on the bed were tossed around, cut open, their feather contents scattered across the hideous object on the bed.

Long Liz Lonergan lay sprawled across her mattress, her throat cut and a poniard thrust into her chest, its hilt protruding obscenely from between her naked breasts. Her arms were flung out in the rough shape of the crux, one hand open, the other tightly clenched into a fist. There was blood everywhere, soaking into the bedclothes.

"Obvious what killed her," Flores stated, reaching forward to pull the knife out.

"Don't touch anything!" Halvar warned. "Zoltan! Is this the way you found her?"

163

The tall guardsman stood by the door, refusing to look inside.

"Yes, Capitán."

"Making rounds?"

Zoltan struggled to keep his voice steady, but he choked on a sob.

"We usually break-the-fast, Liz and me, in my quarters, when she doesn't have an all-nighter. I came for her, saw the door to the crib open, and found her like that, stiff as a board. She's been here all night in the cold, alone! May the Prophet protect her! She was a good woman, in spite of what she did for her bread."

He turned on Halvar, tears leaking from his eyes.

"And you had me chasing that idiot Afrikan! She was here, alone." Sorrow turned to fury. "I was her protector! It was my right to defend her! And thanks to you—"

"You could not have saved her." Eva Hakim spoke from the bed, where she was examining the body. "It is my opinion this woman has been dead for at least twelve hours, which would put the time of death at roughly sundown yesterday. Do you agree, Dr. Moise?"

"I do," Dr. Moise observed from beside the bed as Eva Hakim went over the body carefully.

"She did not go peacefully," the female physician stated. "Her hair is disarranged, her hands are clenched around something." She called to her Local assistant. "Come here, Daria, let us see if we can unlock her fingers."

The Local woman shuddered.

"Bad medicine, to touch the dead."

"I'll do it." Selim leaned over the bed to help. It was no good. The hand stayed firmly shut.

Eva Hakim shook her head sadly.

"The body is stiff. Rigor has set in. Of course, it was exacerbated by the cold—last night there was a hard frost. We must get this poor creature to the House of the Green Crescent and warm the body enough to release whatever she has clutched in her hand."

"There's a bit of something," Selim pointed out.

Both doctors peered at the woman's hand. A tiny scrap of fabric hung from the icy fingers. Selim carefully tugged at it, until it came loose.

"It's lace," she said, holding the fragile item carefully.

"Lace? Franchen-made?" Halvar took the tiny scrap to the window then handed it back to Selim, who folded it into a page of her notebook.

"The woman must have torn it from her assailant," Dr. Moise decided.

"She fought back," Eva Hakim declared. "This hand, the one not clenched, shows marks of the struggle. It is possible that she also marked her attacker."

"So, now we have to find someone with a scratch on their face," Zoltan said, his voice bitter. "And when we do, I'll see that he pays for what he's done to my Liz."

Halvar turned to him.

"When did you last see Long Liz, Guardsman?"

"We left her yesterday, around midday," Zoltan reminded him.

"I know when the rest of us left her. I'm talking to you, Guardsman. You had a, um, special relationship with this woman. When did *you* last see her?"

"I didn't, not yesterday, not after we finished here," Zoltan said, bitterly. "You kept me busy, Capitán, looking for that Shaitan-bred Afrikan. And then, when we found him, we had to take him back to the Rabat, for Dr. Moise to hack into. I didn't get to my quarters until well after sundown, and there was no Liz there."

"And you didn't question why?"

Zoltan shrugged. "Liz was Liz. She might have had a customer, one of the regulars from the madrassa. I don't…didn't…interrupt her. She'd always come to me when she was done."

"Thor's Hammer!" Halvar swore. He turned to the assembled women. "What about you lot? Any of you see this woman yesterday?"

"I seen 'er yesterday at Holy Meal," a blond wench wrapped in a Bretain-made shawl offered. "Prester Nicodemus were right pleased when she dropped a whole silver piece into the offering for Nativity."

"This is Kate," Fergus whispered. "She's a hellcat, but she's honest."

"A whole silver piece!" Halvar repeated. "From the purse Girard left, no doubt. Thanking the Redeemer and Mother Mara for her good fortune."

"She said she'd come into a goodly sum," another woman offered. "Invited us all to Mother Bet's for a Nativity feast."

"Was there that much in Girard's purse?" Halvar wondered.

"It didn't seem like that much," Selim said. "But I suppose, to someone like Long Liz, even just a few imperials would be a fortune."

"There's no silver here now," Flores said, scanning the room.

"Unless Girard had another money pouch, a larger one, that he had with him and she didn't show us," Halvar said, thinking out loud. "There was no money on his person."

"That there silver is what she was killed for," Kate said. "Prester Nicodemus said she was sinning, that she was too proud."

"But he took her silver imperial all the same," the second woman sneered.

"And she told him off, she did!" another woman, a Local in a deerskin skirt and beaded cloth blouse under her fur wrap, put in with a satisfied smirk.

"So, I suppose there's no treat at Mother Bet's tonight?" Kate sighed.

"I'm sorry, ladies," Halvar told them. "Whoever killed Long Liz must have taken her little hoard with them. There's nothing of value here."

The blond woman glared at Zoltan.

"I thought that's what we pay you for, Guardsman! You said you'd keep us safe from thieves! Why should we keep paying, if this is what happens? You said you'd square it with the Scavengers—we pay you, and you keep them satisfied. And now…this!"

"This was no Scavenger," Zoltan protested. "There's a Franchen assassin loose. None of my doing."

Halvar broke into the squabble.

"When did you last see Long Liz?"

The women consulted in Manatas gabble. Then, Kate spoke for the group.

"We was at the Holy Meal together. Then we was headed for Mother Bet's, but Liz stayed behind to give Prester Nicodemus another coin—she said it was for the poor folk that don't have her good fortune, and for the lads he houses at the chapel. They make a bit, running messages here and there, and the good prester gives them lodgings and food.

"He's a good man, Prester Nicodemus, for all that he's Roumi Rite. Says the Redeemer will forgive our sins if we pray and help the chapel. Liz wanted him to pray for the soul of Franz Girard, who was her last customer. He must have been the one paid her those imperials, the way she took on about him."

The Local woman spoke up.

"There was someone waiting by her crib, stopped her in the road."

"Who?" Zoltan demanded.

"It was near dark, I couldn't tell. But Liz said, 'What do *you* want?'"

"So, It sounds as if she recognized this person. Anyone know who it was?" Halvar asked. "Did any of you see him?"

"Just the shadow of a long cape and a big hat," the Local woman said. "It was getting dark. No lanterns lit yet."

"Did you hear anything? Did he speak Franchen, Danic, Erse?" Halvar looked from one shivering female to the other.

"It was dark and cold. Liz took whoever it was into her crib. More fool she!" Kate snarled. "It was her killer we saw!"

"And I wasn't there!" Zoltan cried out.

"There was nothing you could have done," Halvar said, patting the distraught guardsman on the shoulder.

"I was looking for that daft Afrikan all day. I should have been looking after Liz."

"You were following orders," Halvar reminded him. He turned to Flores. "I have all the evidence I need. Arrest ex-Musket-man Devallon. The charge is murder."

"Where do I find him?" Flores looked towards the plaza.

Halvar grinned. "Try the latrine. He should be there, puking his guts out. He drank West Caster cider last night."

"That should keep him busy for a while," Flores said with a snigger.

Halvar turned to the other guardsmen.

"Zoltan, Fergus, you two go to Pearl Street and stand watch on that middle cottage. We should keep our eyes on those milords. Devallon might have been following orders. If so, we want the one who gave them."

"Good idea." Flores nodded agreement.

"In this?" Zoltan gestured at the rapidly lowering sky. "Snow's on the way. No one's going to go out in a storm."

"Bretains are mad," Flores said. "And they're used to nasty weather. Watch the cottage, Zoltan. And if you see anyone leaving it, send for help at once."

Halvar looked up at the sky. There was certainly going to be a storm, very soon. Clouds were piling up at the mouth of the bay. Wind whistled through the gaps between the warehouses and the shacks and buildings. The women held their shawls and furs tighter around them as they headed back to the shelter of the brick house next to Liz's ramshackle crib where they would find warmth, if not comfort.

"Desperate men do desperate things," Halvar added. "Milord Summersby may try to use the snow to cover his escape from Manatas."

"They won't try to leave now," Fergus protested.

"You never can tell what Bretains will take it into their heads to do," Halvar said.

Flores noted the approach of several canoes containing Mahak watchmen.

"It would seem that our Locals have the same idea."

"Firebrand has them stationed on the banks of the East Channel," Halvar observed. "Between your men and his, I want a watch kept on that ship in the harbor. But don't kill anyone else!"

"Unless they try to kill me," Flores warned him. He beckoned to Zoltan and Fergus and swaggered down Maiden Lane.

Halvar glanced up at the sky again; it had taken on a pearly gray sheen. He sent a brief plea to Thor: *Hold off on that storm until I finish this job.*

Then he followed the guardsmen. He needed that visit to the *hammam* before he tackled Devallon.

Chapter 21

A BRIEF SOAK IN THE HAMMAM, A CUP OF mokka and a bowl of maiz mush with added nuts lifted Halvar's spirits considerably. Freshly bathed, barbered and fed, he headed for his office. He looked forward to his interview with that arrogant Franchen musket-man. He wasn't a lad just off the farm anymore. This time, he would be in charge.

The tiny office had been enhanced with the addition of a brazier of hot coals. It did not heat the place to excess, but at least Halvar could no longer see his breath when he exhaled. Selim was waiting for him, eager to impart information.

"You told me to study Captain Girard's personal journal. I copied it all carefully before I passed it on to Leon—I mean, Frater Leonidas. I took it to the fratery in Green Village myself this morning, after I got poor Liz to the House of the Green Crescent, and banged at the door until the doorkeeper brought him out."

"He's still Leon di Vicenza, whatever he chooses to call himself. What does Leon make of it?"

"He was absolutely thrilled. He cooed over the thing as if I'd given him the Great Bird of Paradise as a pet. He's finished his painting of the Redeemer and his followers, and he wanted something else to do besides pray and work in the apothecary's garden."

"And what did he find in this journal?"

A guardsman came in with a mug of steaming hot mokka, set it on the table with a knowing smirk, and headed out again.

"He hasn't really started yet. It's written in some kind of personal code, part Franchen, part Erse, part Old Roumi, even some Danic words, all jumbled together. Leon said it would take time to sort out. What kind of man writes his personal log in code?"

"A careful man," Halvar said, easing into the chair behind the low table that had served the late Tenente Ruiz as a desk. His long legs barely fit underneath, and his feet jutted out, but the seat cushion felt good, and he warmed his hands on the outside of the mug. "Even though this was a personal log, he made sure no one else could read it."

Selim thought this over.

"I still don't understand why anyone would kill him, let alone do it here and now. Why not just do it on the ship?"

"Because the crew were Girard's men," Halvar said after a sip of mokka. "They respected him, even if they didn't like him, because he could get them where they were supposed to go. And he paid them well, too.

"But he brought them here, where they *weren't* supposed to go," Selim pointed out.

"Weren't they?" Halvar asked.

Selim's eyebrows nearly met over her nose.

171

"I thought they were supposed to be sailing to Bella Mara, the new town that Sultan Calvera is building in his Terra Mara territory."

"That's certainly what he told Milord Summersby," Halvar agreed. "But he sent a message to someone before he went to pleasure himself with Long Liz. Perhaps his journal will tell us something different."

Someone rapped at the door. Flores shoved Devallon into the office.

"Like you said, Capitán. In the latrine, puking his guts out." Flores said with malicious glee. He propped himself against the doorjamb, arms folded.

The dapper musket-man was pale and bedraggled. His hair straggled in wisps over his face from under his hat. His mustache and beard were disarranged, hairs sticking out here and there; and there was graying stubble on his cheeks. His boots were mired with the muck of the latrine. There were stains on his jacket and breeches. He eyed Halvar wearily.

"Your bed was comfortable, Dane, but your hospitality was somewhat over-generous."

"I did warn you about the cider," Halvar said. He shoved the only other seat in the room, a three-legged stool, over to Devallon, who collapsed onto it. "Sit down, musket-man, and tell me more about Captain Franz Girard. And don't lie to me this time. I've had enough of your fanciful tales!"

"I beg of you, moderate your voice," Devallon said, wincing at Halvar's strident tone. "I am not completely well this morning."

"Which is why the Prophet was so strict about alcohol," Flores said from his post at the door.

Devallon winced again.

"What do you want to know, Dane?"

"To begin with, why you killed Captain Girard."

Devallon sat up straight on his stool.

172

"I did not! I swear to you, by the Redeemer and all the holy ones of Heaven, I did not!"

"So you say. Our captain knows different," Flores snarled.

"How do you know? What makes you think I was the one who killed him?"

Halvar ticked off points one by one.

"We found fresh ashes and tabac near the body—you smoke a pipe. The weapon used was a Franchen poniard—I've seen you with just such a weapon. You knew where Girard would be—"

"So did his crew," Devallon burst into Halvar's recitation. "They knew he'd be with that whore all night. They take tabac, too. Why not arrest them?"

"Because none of them had a poniard, and none of them had a reason to kill the one man who could get them off Manatas Island," Halvar said.

"Neither did I!" Devallon cried out. "I was Girard's friend! We sailed together from Franchenland to Kibbick! And besides…"

"Yes?" Halvar waited for more.

"It's of no matter. It makes no difference now that he's dead."

"But you were in that alley yesterday morning." Halvar leaned forward again. "You were in the alley, waiting for Girard. You saw him coming, and you drew back into the space between two warehouses, opposite Liz's shack. When he leaned forward to open his breeches, you saw your chance, and stuck your poniard into Girard's neck, very cleanly, very neatly. No blood on your fine jacket or boots."

"Yes, I was in the alley," Devallon confessed. "But I wasn't there to kill Girard. I wanted to have a private word with him, that was all. I knew he'd be all night with the woman, but he'd have to get out at dawn, so I left the Summersby's and followed that path—

Maiden Lane, you call it? And I smoked my pipe, and I waited.

"But someone came up behind me and hit me with something hard. Next thing I knew, I was stuck in a kind of niche between two warehouses, and there were two guardsmen at one end of the alley and some fellow with a wagon and donkey at the other, and Girard between them, all bent over."

"Zoltan and Fergus, on their rounds," Flores said. "And Ibo. He must have passed the body and not noticed in the mist."

"So, you saw Ibo alive," Halvar mused slowly.

"I saw someone leading a donkey cart," Devallon said. "But I couldn't tell you who it was. I could barely see anything in that fog. All I knew was that I mustn't be seen in that alley with a dead man! I made it back to the cottage, where Edgar was raising a fuss about servants. He sent me off to find some."

"Which you did, in the souk," Halvar finished for him.

"Which I did, as you well know." Devallon squared his shoulders. He took off his hat and straightened the bedraggled feather, ran a hand through his tangled hair, and replaced the hat.

"What about Long Liz," Flores snarled.

"What about her? A whore, nothing special about her. Girard liked large, boisterous women. He had a Franchen girl in Kibbick. What was her name? Giselle?" Devallon shook his head, then grimaced at the pain.

"No wife in Franchenland?" Halvar asked.

"If he had one, he never told me."

"What about Long Liz? Why'd you kill her?" Flores stepped closer to the seated prisoner.

Devallon stared at the guardsman, then at Halvar.

"Kill her? I didn't even know her!"

"She must have seen you in that alley," Flores said, taking another step closer to the man on the stool. "You came to her crib last night, just about sundown, while there was still light to see by, and you left your poniard in her heart!"

"I did not!" Devallon looked wildly from Flores to Halvar, truly frightened. "I swear to you, Dane, I did not! I don't kill women."

"Don't you?" Halvar leaned forward, his arms resting on the low table. "Do you recall a certain place in the Dane-March, on the road to Franchenland? I don't even think it had a name, or if it did, it was Something-burg or Something-ville. But it wouldn't let Lovis's army through without paying a toll, and for this, they had to be punished.

"Your company was sent for, and you left winter quarters two weeks before we did. Then the message came for the Free Danes to defend the town against the Musket-men. And we did our best, but there were obstacles—trees down on the road, bad signs that sent us in the wrong direction.

"By the time we got there, we found a town in ruins, bodies all over, the well fouled, and a sword jabbed into the body of the man leading their little resistance band. The sword had the badge of the Franchen Musket-men. They might as well have left a sign: *Resist Lovis, and this will be the consequence.*

"The massacre you told the Sachems about," Selim said.

Halvar could not stop the words pouring out, as if he had lanced a boil to release the foul matter within.

"I saw things that day that kept me awake nights afterward. I saw men lashed to posts that you had used for target practice with those new muskets, except that

175

the aim on those things is so bad you had to shove them in their faces to make sure they were killed. I saw and smelled the bloody heads, blown clean off their necks! I saw a lad, not more than ten, split up the arse, and a little girl, didn't even have breasts, bleeding to death from a dozen men's pizzles.

"I saw a woman, her belly ripped open, and the baby that was inside still hanging from its cord. I was with the gang that cleared them out of the town square and buried what we could, and burned the bits that we couldn't bury properly. Your lot left it to us Danes to clean your mess, Franchen!"

"Orders!" Devallon gasped frantically. "We were told to make an example of the place." He leaned forward to clutch at Halvar's arm. "You understand, Dane, it was orders! You'd have done the same!"

Halvar removed Devallon's grasping hand.

"I was never given such orders. Nor would any of the officers I fought under have given them. Not even in Al-Andalus would someone order such a thing. So, Devallon, don't tell me you wouldn't kill a woman who might be able to point you out as a murderer."

Devallon bit his lips in chagrin.

"All I can say is that I didn't do it. Someone is making it look like I did, but I did not! How could I? You saw me at the taberna. Did I act like someone who had just killed a woman in cold blood?"

"I don't know how you act now, Devallon. I only know what you did when your company and mine were in winter quarters, and your friends took every opportunity to mock at the poor, old-fashioned Danes, with their swords and halberds and pikes, while your company had muskets and cannons.

"I remember how you teased that poor wench at the tavern, the one with the mark on her face, and how you left her in tears. I remember what you did to me when I protested, and you called me a witless oaf. And I remember how you took it out on me when we played kick-the-bladder, and you beat me down, and put your boot in my face, to get a goal.

"And when the game was over, and we were separated, you and your companions had a good laugh about it. So, yes, I think you could kill Long Liz and then be jolly at the taberna. And perhaps, later, you might try to drink yourself into oblivion when it came to you what had done.

"But," Halvar said, frowning in thought, "I don't know why you'd want to kill Girard. And that, Musket-man Devallon, you are going to tell me. Now!"

"How many times must I tell you, I *didn't* kill him!"

"Then who do you think did?" Halvar leaned forward again.

"It could have been one, it could have been the other." Devallon said.. "It's all about those two pairs."

"Milord and Milady Summersby? Their servants?" Halvar was confused.

Devallon shook his head with a derisive laugh.

"Wrong, Dane. Oh, so wrong! Think of those sleeping arrangements. Two bedrooms, two cabins, and who slept with who! There's your answer, Dane. Me? I was the fifth wheel on the carriage! Girard wasn't even in the mixture. Oh, Dane, you have no idea what those four were up to, do you?"

"Why don't you tell me?"

"You're clever, you figure it out." Devallon straightened his hat and smoothed his mustache, under the impression he was back in control of the conversation.

Halvar had had enough.

"Take him to one of the cells," he told Flores. "I want to have a word with Dr. Moise and Eva Hakim about the dead woman, then we'll let Sultan Petrus deal with him at the Little Divan."

Flores jerked Devallon off the stool. Devallon shook the guardsman's hand off, squared his shoulders, and glared at Halvar.

"What happened in the past happened, and is done. What I was then, I am not now. And I did not kill Girard or that woman."

"Or the Afrikan?" Halvar asked.

"What Afrikan?" Devallon looked from Halvar to Flores.

As Devallon preceded Flores out, Halvar asked, "When did you tell Milady about Girard's love life?"

Devallon stopped, halfway into the corridor.

"Tell Charlotte? Why would I do that? It was no business of hers."

"She certainly found out," Halvar said. "She was berating someone in that house, screaming at the top her her lungs. She wasn't happy about it."

Devallon shrugged. "I may have mentioned it to Milord and Edgar, and it's a small house. Easy to over-hear what's said downstairs if you're listening up-stairs."

Halvar stood and followed Flores and his prison-er down the corridor. Flores headed for the cells, Hal-var to the shed across the courtyard. He had a few more questions for the medical examiners before he sent an old soldier to the gallows.

Chapter 22

HALVAR GLANCED UPWARD AS HE CROSSED the courtyard to Dr. Moise's shed. The sky had darkened, but so far, no snow. He settled the fur cap firmly on his head and pulled the collar of his coat closer around his neck. Perhaps he should have used the scarf Yussuf the Tailor had provided with the coat to ease the chafing of the high stiff fabric against his neck.

His eyes adjusted readily to the gloom inside Dr. Moise's sanctuary. The glowing brazier in one corner gave enough heat so the doctor could work without too much discomfort. Two lanterns hung over the table where the body of Ibo lay stretched out, covered only with a cloth over his manly parts.

"Where's Liz?" Halvar asked, looking for the most recent victim of the murderer menacing Manatas.

"Eva Hakim insisted on taking her to the House of the Green Crescent," Dr. Moise said, sounding resentful. "But I made a thorough examination of her body, with or without Eva Hakim's permission."

"And your opinion?" Halvar wished he had been there to see the epic battle between the two most influential medical practitioners on Manatas.

"The woman called Long Liz Lonergan died of several knife wounds, including the final one to her heart." Dr. Moise said. "However, she did not go easily. Eva Hakim will confirm that she must have marked her killer. There was blood under her fingernails, and her face was scratched. There were several shallow wounds in her upper body, across her breasts."

"She went down fighting," Halvar agreed. "What about that one hand? Did you get it open?"

"We found this." Dr. Moise produced a scrap of material. "She must have pulled it off her attacker."

Halvar held the fine mesh close to the lantern.

"Lace," he said. "The rest of what Selim's got in that notebook. It's made in Oropa—Franchenland and Bretain, mostly. Their women make it of fine thread, twisted into patterns."

"Worn by women?" Dr. Moise frowned.

"And men, sometimes," Halvar said. "I don't think this came off anything Long Liz was wearing. It's too fine. Where did I see something like this?"

He closed his eyes to visualize the garments worn by the two Franchen. Did Milord and Milady wear lace on their clothes? Did Devallon?

"It will come to you, I am sure. Now, Don Alvaro, as to this Afrikan." Dr. Moise turned to the body before him. "He was also stabbed in the heart."

"Front or back?" Halvar peered at the body.

"He was facing his killer."

"And he just let himself be stabbed?" Halvar tugged his mustache. "That's not likely, is it?"

"It's not likely, but there it is. The wound is clearly in his chest, just below the rib cage. Very professional, very neat, not much blood. An upward thrust under the breastbone."

"A trained assassin, in other words." Halvar considered his suspects. "One who wears lace and carries a poniard."

"The poniard is a Franchen weapon," Dr. Moise pointed out.

"And Sieur Devallon is Franchen, and he carries a poniard as well as a rapier. But I saw no lace on his shirt, and he claims he did not kill Girard. And he did not even know that Ibo was dead."

"Indeed." The slender Afrikan put a world of meaning into the one word.

"He admits he was in the alley waiting for Girard, but he claims he was struck down, that someone took his poniard and used it to kill Girard. He also claims that he saw someone walking down the alley leading the donkey cart."

"But he cannot say who?"

"There was mist," Halvar reminded the doctor. "And if he was struck on the back of the head, he might not have been seeing very clearly. I've got him in a cell, Dr. Moise. If you can find the time, you can examine him to see if he has a lump or bruise on the back of his head."

"That I can do." Dr. Moise said. "One more thing I can tell you, Don Alvaro. This Afrikan was probably dead well before he was put into the latrine. I suspect he saw the murder of Girard and was attacked before he could understand what he saw."

"They say he was a halfwit," Halvar said. "So, perhaps he didn't realize the killer was dangerous."

"A man with a bloody dagger in his hand not dangerous?" Dr. Moise sniffed. "He must have been a halfwit indeed."

Halvar tugged on his mustache again.

"I just remembered where I saw lace," he said. "And I know why poor Ibo didn't recognize a murderer when he saw one."

He dashed out the door into the courtyard to see Flores and two guardsmen emerging from the central tower.

"We've got our killer locked down tight," Flores told him. "Devallon's chained to the wall. He'll meet his end soon enough."

"Devallon's not the killer," Halvar said. "Thor's Hammer, what now?"

Three men fought for precedence at the gate—a green-coated Guardsman, a Mahak in a hunting shirt, and Rachev the Scavenger in his ragtag caftan. All were yelling for Halvar's attention. Fergus, the Guardsman, shoved the Mahak aside and scrambled into the courtyard to salute Tenente Flores.

"Tenente! We've been watching the houses on Pearl Street, like you said. There's something doing with the Bretain toffs! They've got a gang of Afrikans hauling stuff out of the house, down to the waterfront."

"Stealing the furniture out of the house!" Flores was aghast. "That's not right!"

"That a Bretain Milord should stoop to thievery?" Halvar agreed. He turned to Rachev. "That's your job, isn't it? Removing the contents of empty houses?"

"We never got that stuff out," Rachev sputtered. "Too heavy to lift! I'm here for poor Ibo. We want to give him a proper burial before the ground gets too hard, and we have to wait till the spring thaw."

"You can have him whenever you like." Dr. Moise had emerged from his shed. "But you'd better do it quickly."

Halvar turned to the Mahak.

"What's *your* message?"

"Watchmen see sailors on small boat. They carry things to round ship."

"They're trying to leave port." Halvar loped out the gate, motioning for the guards to follow him. "And They're helping those Bretains to escape! You, Mahak, get back to the waterfront. Stop those sailors, but don't kill them. Flores, you and Fergus follow me. Selim, alert the sultan's guards, send them to the waterfront."

Halvar headed towards the East Channel as the first flakes of snow drifted down from the leaden sky.

Chapter 23

HALVAR DASHED DOWN THE PATH TO THE
waterfront without waiting to see whether his troops
followed or not. Large flakes of wet snow fell on the
stones under his feet, turning them treacherous as he
slid down the slope to the East Channel.

A chorus of squawks and honks greeted him at
the crossing of Pearl Street, punctuated by the bleat-
ing of a goat and the shrill cries of the resident rooster. Halvar stopped, panting for breath. He was up to
his knees in poultry!

"Thor's Hammer! Who let the chickens out?"

The Danic and Bretain residents of Pearl Street
were out in force, trying to corral the fluttering hens,
while Zoltan and two guardsmen tried to avoid the
menacing wings and beak of a large gander defend-
ing his territory.

"Out of the way, lummox!" The stout Danic woman shoved Zoltan aside as she shooed hens around him towards the chicken yard.

"It was the woman," Zoltan tried to explain, lifting his feet as the infuriated hens pecked at his boots and their keeper made clucking noises at them. The rooster made its presence known with a series of piercing calls from the top of the henhouse.

"What woman? Milady?" Halvar dodged the horns of the goat, which was evading the milkmaid

"I don't know which of them it was," Zoltan said. "Me and Fergus was watching the house, like you ordered. The two men left, and I sent Fergus to tell you. Then the two women come out, and the one in the blue cloak opened the gate to the henyard and yelled at the birds, and they all come out. And the goat got the idea—"

"What's this about the furnishings?"

"That was something else. That servingman, Edgar, come along with a couple of Afrikans and a donkey cart. They got the table and the chairs out of the house —heavy stuff they was—and they loaded them onto the cart and headed down the path to the waterfront. That's when I tried to stop them, because I thought they was stealing them. That stuff goes with the house, it don't belong to Milord, no matter what that Bretain stiff-back says!"

"But you couldn't stop them?" Halvar was ready to throttle the man.

"There was three of the Afrikans, counting the one that was already hired in the house—big fellows, and one of me," Zoltan protested. "I couldn't fight all of them. I did what we was told to do—send for reinforcements."

"Two men, two women, you said. Milady and her servant?"

Halvar tried to assess what was going on.

The chickens fluttered around his feet, squawking and pecking at anything they could see. The gander and goose flapped their wings. The goat bleated.

"Didn't sound like no servant to me," Zoltan said. "Cussing a storm, she was, and giving orders. Told the Afrikans to load the cart, told the other wench to look sharp."

"The one in red," Fergus added.

Halvar willed himself to be calm.

"The wagon with the furnishings. Where is it now?"

"Down the path." Fergus pointed to the narrow lane that led to the waterfront.

"Follow me!"

Halvar waved at the Guardsmen and raced down the path. They got halfway along then had to stop their headlong rush to the waterfront. The cart had tipped over, the heavy chairs and table lying across the road. The cart itself was wedged between the outside stairs of the Mermaid Taberna and the latrines, making an effective barrier for anyone trying to go down the hill to the waterfront. There was no sign of the Afrikans or their donkey.

"Thor's Hammer!" Halvar swore. He clambered over the barrier, reaching the outside stairs to his quarters. "Get rid of this stuff!" he shouted down to the men on the path. "And get to the waterfront as quickly as you can."

"What are you going to do?" Flores yelled back.

"I'm going to stop that killer from leaving Manatas!"

Halvar bounded up the stairs, ran through his rooms, and down the inside stair to the main room of the taberna. He ignored the startled cries of the few

patrons of the taberna, shoved past Hannes, and darted into the plaza.

Firebrand was waiting with his Mahak.

"What took you so long?"

"They tried to block the way," Halvar explained
between gasps. "Where are they?"

Firebrand pointed to the dock.

"The sailors have taken their leader to the ship in
one rowing boat. There is one more for the rest of them."

"Milord and Milady?"

"No man. Two women."

Halvar strode across the plaza; he could now make
out two blobs of color against the white snow.

"Stop, in the name of the Calif Don Felipe of Al-
Andalus!" he roared.

He headed for the dock, where Dame Brigitte and
Milady Summersby were struggling to get into the rowboat while two of the *Belle Fleur*'s crew worked the
oars to hold the boat steady, and two more tried to
guide the would-be passengers into the bobbing craft.

"The calif can go piss on himself in Hades!" The
woman in the blue cloak turned to face Halvar. The
wind blew the hood away from her face. She had applied rouge with a liberal hand, but the snowflakes
melted on her skin, and Halvar could see the angry red
streak under the paint.

"Dame Brigitte. Such foul language for a respectable
Franchen matron," he admonished her, as he reached
the end of the dock. He looked around for a weapon
more lethal than his dagger and found none. He hoped
it would not come to hand-to-hand combat with Dame
Brigitte. He had a healthy respect for the fighting skill
of Franchen women.

Below, the water of the East Channel churned, and
waves slapped at the piers of the wooden dock.

"Brigitte! Where is Andres! We have to wait for Andres!" Milady Summersby called from the boat.

"If it's Devallon you mean, he's at the Rabat," Halvar told her. "Get out of that boat, Milady, and come back to the Rabat. It's dangerous out there!"

"More dangerous here," Brigitte spat. "Charlotte, stay where you are! I'll take care of this lout!"

She swung around again; something fell onto the dock with a metallic chink. Halvar took two more strides and grabbed at the blue cloak that was weighted by something sewn into the hem.

The Franchen woman twisted, sending the cloak swirling across Halvar's shins. Whatever weighed the hem struck him, sending him off-balance. The delay gave Brigitte time to scoot to the end of the dock, where the boatmen struggled with the ropes that held the dinghy to the dock.

Halvar caught her just as she reached the wooden ladder at the end of the pier. He grabbed for her cloak again to haul her back. She whirled, landing hard slaps on each of his cheeks, following that with a blow with the side of her hand to the bridge of his nose.

His eyes filled with tears. Halvar reeled back, his hand on his dagger. He didn't want to have another woman's death on his hands, but she gave him no choice.

He lunged forward, and felt his feet slipping on the icy surface of the pier. He landed flat on his back as Brigitte clambered down the ladder to the boat below.

"Row, you arseholes, you shitheads! Row!"

Then, the woman's harsh screams were swallowed up by the slapping waves and the whistling wind.

The rowboat parted from the dock just as Flores and his guards trotted up to help Halvar to his feet. Firebrand and his Mahaks joined them as they stood, helplessly watching the boat bob on the choppy waves, the blue cloak and the red cloak obscured by white flakes.

Halvar turned to Firebrand, but the Mahak had already anticipated the order.

"I will not go out in a canoe in such water," he said firmly. "Nor will I order my people to do it. It is madness. They will surely overturn."

"No, they won't!"

The voice from behind reminded Halvar there was one more factor in this increasingly complicated plot to deal with. He turned to face Milord Summersby.

"Milady is taking her chances with the waves. I hope you won't be so foolish as to try and join her."

"Charlotte will be safer on that ship than here in this miserable excuse for a town," Summersby snarled.

"And you expect to join her?" Halvar looked at the dhow belayed to the pier. "Are you thinking to sail this dhow into the bay? Or maybe hire one of the Mahak to paddle you to the ship?"

"Edgar has found another boatman," Summersby informed him. "They should be here at any moment. I've paid him in good silver, fresh from the Imperial Mint."

"Some things can't be bought," Halvar said. He advanced on Summersby, hand on dagger. "And some things are worth more than money."

Summersby edged away, his hand on the hilt of his sword.

"Like honor?" he sneered.

"Like keeping one's word," Halvar agreed. He had to keep the Bretain talking, and get off that slippery wooden pier. "How much is your life worth, Milord Summersby?"

Summersby took a pace forward, forcing Halvar back.

"I *will* get to the ship!"

"You will not."

"Are *you* going to stop me?" Summersby drew his sword. "With your little knife, Dane?"

"I have friends," Halvar said. "Look behind you, Milord. The Manatas Town Guard and the Sultan's men have arrived, in spite of your blockade."

"And we don't like murderers, especially not 'noble' Bretains." Flores advanced with his halberd, point down, to Summersby's right.

"Nor do the Mahak," Firebrand stated flatly, standing on Summersby's left, his war-club at the ready.

"I don't want you dead, Milord," Halvar said, stepping carefully off the pier. "But you must come with me to the Rabat. There are questions that must be answered."

"Not by me!" Summersby drew his sword and rushed Halvar. "Edgar! To me!"

"Henry!" More men appeared in the snow, armed with clubs and knives. "I found some more men, sailors, they have a boat—"

Halvar grabbed Flores's halberd.

"You with the Bretain! This is Capitán Halvar Danske of the Manatas Town Guard. These men are trying to escape the Sultan's justice! Lay down your weapons! Tenente Flores, get that servant, Edgar. Get him to the Rabat, alive. You can hurt him, but whatever you do, don't kill him."

"Henry! Get to the ship!" Edgar cried out. "Never mind me, you have to get to the ship!"

"Not possible," Halvar gritted out. He heard the sounds of battle behind him, grunts and shouts and the smack of wood on leather, and tried to ignore them. He had to concentrate on the one person in front of him.

Step by step, he moved off the wooden dock, feeling the bricks of the plaza under his feet. He used the halberd to drive Summersby back, poking the axe-head at the man's belly, trying to avoid the blade swinging towards him.

"Give it up, Summersby. You're outnumbered and outmatched."

Summersby did not bother to respond. Instead, he lunged, trying to reach Halvar with the point of his blade. Halvar felt a sting on his cheek and leaped back, swinging the halberd to deflect the sword.

It was an uneven match on the face of it, Halvar's long pole against the length of the sword blade; but Summersby's foppish exterior hid a practiced swordsman. He flicked at Halvar again and again, trying to goad the other man into making a useless headlong rush that would take him within reach of the sword's edge.

Halvar had to rely on defensive maneuvers while trying to move Summersby to where the guards could grab him. Above all, he didn't want a repetition of his first deadly fight on Manatas, where he had pushed Tenente Gomez into the Great River. He had to keep the Bretain alive.

Whereas Summersby definitely wanted to kill him!

They circled, sword against axe-head, as the snow began to pile up against the piers of the dock.

"They've reached the ship!" Edgar yelled suddenly.

The sounds of battle stopped. The guardsmen and sailors turned to look for the hulk of the round ship, just visible in the veil of falling snow.

Summersby spun about, dropping his guard. Halvar stepped forward and swung the halberd to knock the rapier out of the Bretain's hand. Flores grabbed Summersby by one arm as the Bretain stared across the bay.

"Flores! Hold him fast!"

Summersby wrenched out of Flores's grasp and headed for a canoe beached next to the piers. Firebrand blocked his way, war-club in hand.

"I will not kill you. Not yet."

Halvar peered through the snow. He could barely make out the *Belle Fleur* rolling in the bay. The red cloak and the blue could be seen against the brown side of the ship. The dinghy was being hauled up, one end at a time. The person in the red cloak, smaller and lighter, clung to the rope ladder, while the heavier person in the blue cloak was being tossed about as the dinghy bumped upwards.

"They've got her!" Summersby shouted in triumph as the red cloak disappeared, apparently pulled over the ship's rail.

"Not quite," Halvar said, pointing to the blue cloak.

The rowboat had come loose from one of the ropes tying it to its mooring davit. Brigitte clung to the edge of the craft, reaching for the slippery rope ladder, her weighted cloak impeding her attempts to reach it. With a cry that could be heard across the bay, she fell into the bay.

"The Three Old Women are always fair," Halvar declared. "Just as she killed to get those silver imperials, they have killed her." He pointed to a gleaming object on the pier. "They were sewn into the lining of that blue cloak. She could have saved herself by losing it, but she could not leave her silver coins."

"But Charlotte is safe," Summersby said. "And the ship will sail."

192

"Not in this storm," Halvar declared. "No sailor will go aloft in this."

"The ship—it's leaving!" Flores pointed to *Belle Fleur*, which was moving majestically toward the gap between the Long and Round Islands.

"They've cut the anchor," Summersby said with a satisfied nod. "Michel can steer through the gap."

"They expect the current to carry them across the bay," Firebrand said. "But there are currents in this water they do not know."

Halvar watched with dismay as the ship started to turn, caught by one of the currents around the small islands that dotted the bay. He could almost make out the rudder as Michel struggled to hold the ship steady.

"They're going too close to the shore!" someone yelled.

"There are rocks." The Mahak canoe paddler, Muskrat, asserted. "I know these waters. You cannot take a round ship close to the shore. It will break up on the rocks."

"And what of the people on board?" Halvar asked, unable to take his eyes from the sight of the ship in distress.

"The Kanarsee live on this part of the Long Island." That was the other canoe paddler, Seulemon. "They are my people. They will take what they can from the ship. It is their way."

Halvar watched, furious at his own impotence to stop the tragedy. The snow blocked the scene from view, but he could hear the thump and crash as the *Belle Fleur* came to a sudden, juddering halt on the unseen rocks beneath the tumbling waves.

"And so is made manifest the Will of Ilha, may his name be praised," Flores said finally. "What do we do now, Capitán?"

Halvar wiped ice off his mustache and shook snow off his fur hat.

"We take these two back to the Rabat and let Sultan Petrus decide what to do with them."

Chapter 24

IT WAS A LONG, SLOW SLOG BACK TO THE RA-
bat. Two guards preceded Flores, who marched Summersby and Edgar triumphantly up the hill, evidence
of the efficiency of the Manatas Town Guard. A few
scavengers who were already hard at work sweeping
the snow off the path with brooms hooted and jeered
as Flores told them the Bretains were going to get
what was coming to them for the murder of poor Ibo.

The donkey cart and its load of furniture had been
shifted to make a narrow path up the hill. The heavy
table and chairs were stored under the stairs that led
to Halvar's rooms, but that did nothing to protect the
fine wood from the snow and wind. By the time Halvar reached it, the path from the waterfront to Pearl
Street was slushy mush, treacherously slippery un-
derfoot. He felt the squishy muck oozing into his boots.

By now, Pearl Street was free of poultry. The goat bleated resentfully from its pen; the hens and geese clucked and squawked from their roosts. At least that part of Manatas had been restored to order.

The walls of the Rabat loomed over the returning squad; Halvar could see the torches on either side of the gate, lit in the gloom of early twilight. It was the End-of-Fast Feast Day, he remembered. All the mokka-shops that had been closed would be open again. Students at the Madrassa, merchants who had stayed the winter, all the craftsmen and vendors at the souk —all would be out tonight, celebrating the final day of the fast.

Somewhere beyond the souk, in the Yehudit quarter, there would be lights and feasting to commemorate a long-ago victory over a deadly foe and the dedication of a holy temple.

In Green Village, there would be bonfires, and songs and celebrations to mark the return of the sun to the heavens and the promise of spring. Good would always triumph over Evil, Light over Darkness, and the sun would shine again.

All this was very fine, Halvar thought bitterly, but once again, true victory over evil had eluded him. *The Three Old Women must be laughing at me*, he thought. *They show me a villain, then take her away.*

He plodded doggedly along, turning everything he had seen or heard in the last two days over in his mind. Devallon, Milord and Milady Summersby, Edgar and Brigitte…and Captain Girard—how did it all fit? Silver imperial coins, land grants in Kibbick and Terra Mara. Two cabins, two bedrooms…and a long-legged whore?

He stopped short, nearly losing sight of Flores and his prisoners in the snow. Zoltan bumped into him from behind.

"That's it!" Halvar said. Now, how to prove it?

When they reached the gates of the Rabat, Zoltan turned to face him.

"With your permission, Capitán, it's the end of our shift. Fergus and me, we want to get back to our own digs."

"You don't stay in barracks?" Halvar had assumed all the Guardsmen would take advantage of lodgings and food at the calif's expense.

"We got a room at a place on the waterfront," Fergus explained. "It's handier. And they'll wake for Long Liz—we should be there, to show respect."

Halvar nodded. "Go, then. You've done enough for one day." He followed Flores through the gates and looked his prisoners over.

"What shall I do with these two?" Flores asked, shoving the two Bretains forward.

"Take them to my office. I want a few words with them. Then find Selim—I want the lad to record what goes on."

The man at the gate looked them over as they trudged into the courtyard.

"Looks like you fellows have had a good time."

"Got two, lost two," Flores snarled. "What's happening here?" He looked around the courtyard. Lanterns hung from the cressets that usually held torches.

"Sultan's feasting," the Guardsman responded. "Don Alvaro, I am told to tell you to present yourself as soon as possible. Most of the worthies who were invited sent their regrets, couldn't come in the snow, but the Excellent Sultan has sent extra rations for us Guardsmen, and a measure of cider as well, in honor of the Prophet, may his name be praised."

Halvar looked down at his sullied coat. He couldn't go back to his own rooms to change now. He would have to get cleaned up as best he could. Perhaps he could find another Guardsman's coat large enough to fit his broad shoulders and extra height.

"Send word to the Excellent Sultan that I will come as soon as I have finished with the two prisoners," he told the Guardsman. "Flores, you're free as soon as you bring Selim to me. And get Devallon, too. Let's see if there's really honor among thieves."

"With permission, Capitán, I want to hear what these two have to say." Flores prodded them with the butt of his halberd. "And that Franchen? What's his part in this mess?"

"A question I think I can answer," Halvar said. "But I have to be sure before I bring my findings to the sultan. Let them wait a bit while I sort myself out in the office, then bring them to me."

The office was damp and chilly, the coals in the brazier barely smoldering. One of the guards brought some more twigs and set the charcoal blazing again, and when the room was warm enough Halvar removed his coat and shook the drops of melted snow off his fur hat. He took his seat behind the low desk as the two bedraggled Bretains were thrust into the room by the guards, followed by Flores and Devallon.

Selim arrived decked out in a blue silk coat embroidered with stylized flowers, fastened with silver braid toggles across an increasingly large chest. Her braids were tucked under a blue silk turban, which had been pinned with a sapphire brooch.

Halvar greeted her with a grin, which she returned. She was dressed for a festive occasion, but she was much happier taking notes in his office than sitting with the women at her father's feast.

"Ah! Here is our recorder. Selim, sit and take down exactly what is said."

She eyed him, knowing he would not ordinarily appear in public without a coat or jacket. To see him in his shirt was totally unexpected. She took in the bedraggled Bretains in their soiled finery and touched her turban to show that at least one person in the room had some respect for the End-of-Fast holiday.

"You were in another fight," she accused, taking in Halvar's cuts and bruises and his soiled coat.

"And I didn't invite you. Sorry for that, but I didn't think I'd need a secretary when I went off to chase criminals. Still, you are here now, and I want you to take down all that is said, so no clever advocate can later claim I was not completely fair with these Bretains."

He eyed the prisoners.

"Milord Henry Summersby, Sieur Andres Devallon, and Edgar—What is your family name?"

"Norris," Edgar said, sullenly. "I am Edgar Norris, servant to Milord Henry Summersby."

"And no doubt much more, but that's not my affair," Halvar said with a malicious grin. "Write down that I do not accuse Milord Henry Summersby of the murders of Captain Franz Girard, Ibo the Afrikan, or the prostitute known as Long Liz Lonergan. Nor do I accuse Heer Edgar Norris, and I absolve Sieur Andres Devallon, also."

"Of course we didn't kill them," Summersby exclaimed. "I could have told you that, if you'd bothered to listen."

Halvar went on. "However, while you did not do the deed, you sheltered the one who did, and under Sharia law, that makes you just as guilty."

"But…if not them, then, who?" Flores asked.

"We're missing two of their party," Halvar pointed out. "Milady Charlotte Summersby, and the woman called Dame Brigitte."

"Charlotte? What of Charlotte?" Devallon burst out. "Not dead?"

"To our knowledge, not dead. Probably in the hands of the Algonkin, and as far as I've been told, they don't kill prisoners. They set them to work, but they don't kill them." Halvar reassured him. "She tried to escape on the *Belle Fleur*, which went aground on the rocks of the Long Island. According to my Local sources, the Algonkin and Oropan settlers will rescue anyone they can from such wrecks. As soon as this storm is over, I will send one of the Locals to find out how she is faring."

Halvar watched the three men closely. Devallon closed his eyes and murmured something in Franchen that might have been a prayer to the Redeemer. Milord and Edgar seemed unmoved.

"You don't seem unduly worried about your bride, Milord," he remarked. "Strange, considering you've only been married a short time, and you paid a considerable sum to remove her from Kibbick.

"Which leads me to wonder. Just how attached are you to Milady Summersby? One would think you had some great affection for her. Or was it for the silver and land that came with her?"

Summersby said nothing, just bit his lip and glared at Devallon.

"He's guessing," the old soldier said.

"I am," Halvar said. "And what I guess is this—that this whole mess started in Franchenland, when someone—perhaps it was you, Devallon, or perhaps it was Dame Brigitte—heard that Lovis Younger was going to send women to Nova Mundum, with silver and land grants, on a ship called *Belle Fleur*. One, or both of you, approached a young woman named Charlotte. I don't know her family name, but she's now called Milady Summersby."

"Her family name was Besson," Devallon provided.

'Write that down, Selim—Charlotte Besson. I had a feeling you might know her better than you claimed, Devallon. Your given name is Andres, is it not?"

Devallon nodded. "Yes, my given name is Andres. And, yes, I knew Charlotte Besson as a relation. A distant relation, some kind of cousin of my mother, fallen on hard times thanks to the wars in the Dane-march. How did you guess?"

"She called you by your given name, Andres. No one else even knows it. And you don't always remember to call her by her title of Milady. As for the woman called Dame Brigitte—another relation?"

Once again Devallon nodded.

"Not a relation, but a close...friend."

"Of yours, or Charlotte's?"

Devallon shrugged.

"Both, I suppose. Where *is* Dame Brigitte? Did she get to the ship?"

"She reached the ship but fell into the bay, and the coins she had sewn into the hem of her cloak weighed her down. She might have saved herself if she had let go of them. Her greed was her downfall."

Devallon made the sign of the crux.

"Greed," he repeated. "Her besetting sin."

"And it was greed that made Dame Brigitte do what she did. First she killed Girard, then Ibo, and finally Liz, all for the sake of silver imperials."

Flores gasped. "You mean *she* killed Girard? But why?"

"Because he took money she thought belonged to her, by right."

"But that's ridiculous!" Milord sputtered. "I gave Girard the silver imperials that came with Charlotte as her dowry."

201

"But she was supposed to share them with Dame Brigitte for getting her onto the ship in the first place. Dame Brigitte must have known Girard in Franchenland. Otherwise, how would she have known which ship the women would be on, and the circumstances surrounding them? And how else could she have gotten the position of matron, which would ordinarily have gone to one of the sorors of the Roumi Rite?

"I'm not Roumi Rite myself, but I know how careful they are about young women, about guarding the purity of prospective brides. A bawd like Dame Brigitte would need a powerful advocate to get a position of authority like that. Who better than the captain of the ship bringing the girls to Kibbick?"

Devallon nodded. "Clever reasoning, Dane. You're right, Girard knew Dame Brigitte. He was one of her best customers when he was in port."

"And possibly more than a customer," Halvar suggested. "Girard liked large, strong women with bad tempers and salty tongues. Dame Brigitte certainly fit that description. And it would explain the viciousness of her attack on Long Liz, not at all like the neat way she dispatched the Afrikan with one thrust directly into the heart."

"But Girard had nothing to do with her on either of the voyages," Devallon pointed out. "I was there. She kept to her cabin on the way to Kibbick, and again, out of Kibbick, all the way here."

"That was her mistake," Halvar said. "I don't think she considered that she might become a victim of the seasickness that attacks some passengers. The heaving and rolling of the boat was too much for her."

"And Charlotte was able to escape her vigilance," Devallon filled in. "But she wasn't the sort to appeal to Girard, so she waited until we reached Kibbick and took what she could."

"Which was you, Milord." Halvar turned to Summersby, who had been taking in the revelations with gasps of outrage.

"I knew nothing of this!" Summersby protested. "Charlotte…Milady Summersby…told me she was a girl of good family whose father had lost all in a business deal gone sour."

"And that may well be true," Halvar said before Devallon could refute the claim. "But you are not a man who cares much for women in any case, are you? You already had a lover—Edgar Norris. But you cannot admit your relationship to the world, so you married Charlotte Besson and took her silver imperials and her land grant.

"But there was a small snag—the grant was in Kibbick, in Franchen territory, and it wasn't cleared land but forest. You didn't want that, so you traded your forest in Kibbick for a farm in Terra Mara, where the land is already cleared.

"So, you then hired the largest ship in port, the *Belle Fleur*, to take you there. And Girard, who wanted to go to Terra Mara for his own reasons, took your silver imperials and headed south."

"And made port, first in Bos-Town, then here," Summersby put in.

"So I've been told. You had some trouble in Bos-Town, and didn't want to come here, but Girard was in charge of the ship, and here he would come."

Summersby pouted.

"I ordered him to sail south, but he told me there was a storm brewing. That there was a good taberna where Milady and I would be well-accommodated, and that we would sail south as soon as the storm was over. He didn't tell me about any other business he had."

Halvar eyed the Bretain thoughtfully.

"He *wouldn't* tell you what he was up to,. He was after a bigger sum than any you could have given him, if what I think he was up to is right.

"Captain Girard loved two things—money and women. Having obtained the first, he wanted the second, and that was his undoing. He decided to revisit an old acquaintance, Long Liz Lonergan, and he paid her with the silver imperials Milord Summersby had given him. The silver imperials that were originally brought to Kibbick on behalf of Charlotte Besson—"

"Who was supposed to hand them to Dame Brigitte as a fee for connecting her with a noble Bretain milord," Devallon finished slowly.

"So, the whore was killed for the silver?" Milord was still trying to understand what had happened. "But, how did Dame Brigitte know about her?"

"That's the trouble with old soldiers," Halvar said with a sigh. "They have a crude sense of humor, and they like to gossip more than old women. Devallon was friendly with Girard. I'm sure they exchanged some spicy stories during the long nights on the voyage from Franchenland. Did Girard tell you about Long Liz, Devallon?"

"Again, Dane, you're right. We exchanged a few reminiscences, and when we came close to Manatas, Girard told me he had some business to attend to here, and that he'd do some of it with the tallest whore on the island."

"And you told Milord and Heer Edgar," Halvar said. "And I doubt you whispered this tasty tale—you have a good, loud voice, Devallon. Dame Brigitte must have heard you say you were going to find Girard as soon as it was light. She followed you to Maiden Lane, hit you on the head with a brick or stone, took your poniard, and stabbed Girard.

"I don't know if she'd planned to attack Liz next, but once again, the Three Old Women took charge. Along came Ibo the Afrikan with his donkey cart. He didn't realize what he was seeing, but *she* didn't know he was a halfwit. She stabbed him, loaded him into the cart, and took the path that led to the latrine. She propped him up and went back to the cottage, leaving two dead bodies and one live one to be accused of the murder."

"Which we did!" Flores thumped his halberd on the floor.

"But there were reasons I didn't think you'd killed Girard, Devallon. It didn't ring true, somehow. Yes, I knew what you'd done in that town, but that was under orders, as you said, , with others. There was no reason for you to attack Girard, especially not that way.

"Furthermore, you're a tall man—as tall as me—and Girard was stabbed by someone shorter than he. Then, you told me you'd been struck on the head. If you were lying, you'd have made up a much better tale."

"Thank you for that, Dane…I think."

"What's more, you don't wear lace on your shirt."

"Can't afford it, don't like it," Devallon grumbled.

"True. And you couldn't have been the one to accost Long Liz last night, after Holy Meal. You were waiting for me at the Mermaid Taberna, and I'm sure there are a dozen men who will tell me they saw you there well before sundown, including Hannes Zilberstam. So, I have to release you, Devallon. You did not kill anyone. At least, not here on Manatas."

Devallon bowed ironically.

"But what made you suspect Brigitte?" Summersby asked.

"It took some time, I will admit it. I didn't want to think that a woman could be a practiced assassin."

Halvar said. "For a time, I thought the killer might be you, Milord, or your man, Edgar Norris. You might have killed Girard if he threatened to tell of your relationship, especially in a place like Terra Mara, where Roumi Rite is the principal religion.

"And if Ibo had seen either of you, you might have killed him to stop him from identifying you. But neither of you would have a reason to attack Long Liz, who hadn't witnessed the murder of Girard; and neither of you has a scratch on his face, as you would have if you'd attacked her.

"Dame Brigitte had the coins, she had the scratch, she had the motive, and she had your poniard, Devallon. I noticed it was missing when I looked your gear over last night."

"I thought I'd left it at the cottage," Devallon muttered, shamefaced.

Halvar went on. "Dame Brigitte had the lace, on her cap. She fought me like any ruffian in a Parigi dive. And she has met her end, pulled down by her own greed."

He studied the three men in front of him.

"Milord Summersby, Heer Norris, you are not murderers. True, you resisted arrest, but it's understandable, under the circumstances. For now, I will let you go back to your cottage. I only hope there's something left in it for you to sit on. The Scavengers will have picked it clean again."

He turned to Selim. "Have you written all that?"

"Yes, Don Alvaro."

"Tenente Flores, you will bear witness that I have not intimidated or threatened these prisoners in any way?"

"You've been gentler to them than I would," Flores growled.

"Then, let us attend the sultan's End-of-Fast Feast," Halvar decided. "We will provide some unusual entertainment, but it will be fitting to end one year and greet the new sun properly."

With that, he brushed the last of the muck off his coat, put the fur hat over his Danic cap, and prepared to attend a party.

Chapter 25

SULTAN PETRUS HAD SPARED NO EXPENSE TO
make his End-of-Fast Feast a grand occasion. The old
soldier sat in his favorite chair, which had been
placed near his new stove, his ivory leg propped up
on a footstool.

He was draped in a silk caftan with an embroidered hem and cuffs. His fingers were adorned with
rings, his turban sported a large emerald brooch, and
his beard had been carefully trimmed and dyed with
henna.

The bare walls of the sultan's room had been covered with printed kutton cloths, as much to keep out
the chill wind as for decoration. Lanterns hung over
the torch cressets, adding a warm glow to the otherwise grim room.

The large round table that usually dominated the
center of the room had been moved aside to allow

several smaller tables to be placed in front of the assembled guests. These held trays of savory snacks and sweet pastries, along with glass goblets and ewers filled with an amber liquid that might be the ever-present cider, and a darker fluid that could even be wine.

Halvar paused in the doorway to assess the company. Even without the presence of the merchants and clerics who'd had to decline the sultan's hospitality due to the weather, the room seemed to be uncomfortably crowded. The Afrikan and Andalusian servants huddled against the wall near the stairs that led to the harem. On the other side of the room, Lady Ayesha lolled on a pile of cushions behind the new stove, luxuriating in its warmth, surrounded by her little band of servants. The Maya girl sat next to her; the Local nursemaid held Baby Zuzu, who had been put into a deerskin bag laced onto a wooden board that could be propped up against a wall or carried on a woman's back. Behind her stood two Afrikan slaves, shivering in thin kutton tunics and trousers.

Halvar wished he'd had the time to go back to his rooms and change into something more fitting for a grand feast. At least he'd had a bath and a shave that morning. He approached the sultan and salaamed.

"I greet you, Excellent Sultan, and give you the felicitations of this glorious day," he said in his most precise Arabi. "Forgive me if I am not suitably dressed for this auspicious occasion and this grand company."

Sultan Petrus waved him forward

"My man tells me you've been busy with more important matters than clothing. I was watching from this window. I saw the ship in the harbor run aground. How did that come about?"

"I think the first mate, the man called Michel Primero, wanted to turn the ship into the storm," Halvar said. "But Ilha, may his name be praised, had other plans."

"And the murderer of the Franchen captain, and the Afrikan? You captured him?"

"That, too, was taken out of my hands," Halvar admitted. "And it was a woman, not a man, who killed them both. As well as a woman on Maiden Lane," he added. "The murderess was dragged into the water by silver sewn in her cloak, which silver was the reason for her evil deeds. As the Holy Book has it, love of money is at the root of evil."

"So said the Prophet, may his name be blessed," Sultan Petrus corrected him. "So, Capitán Don Alvaro, what of the Bretain Milord and Milady? Are we rid of them, too?"

"Not quite," Halvar said. "Milord Henry Summersby has done nothing wrong by sharia law. The woman who called herself Dame Brigitte was not his servant but his wife's, and she acted on her own, without telling anyone of her plans. Heer Devallon knew nothing of those plans, either."

"I thought there was evidence to arrest him." Sultan Petrus shifted in his chair. "Tenente Flores, didn't your men arrest this Devallon? He was in the cells today, yelling his head off, claiming he was a subject of Imperator Lovis and not bound by the laws of Al-Andalus."

"But I have proved to my satisfaction, and to the satisfaction of any advocate or *cadi*, that he did not kill the woman called Long Liz Lonergan," Halvar said. "And so, Excellent Sultan, he, too, must be set free."

Sultan Petrus grunted his displeasure.

"Mmmph! Emir Achmet won't like it."

"Emir Achment's Scavengers will have their hands full of snow," Halvar joked. "Give them brooms and shovels and set them to clearing the roads after this storm is over, and pay them well, and they'll forget about Ibo. His killer has met Ilha's justice. So be it."

Sultan Petrus's face relaxed into a jovial smile.

"And so, all is well," he declared. "Capitán Don Alvaro, once again you have demonstrated the wisdom of our esteemed calif, Don Felipe, may he rule long, in giving you this position. Join us in our festivities! I have food and drink, please, my friends—partake!"

The servants clustered around the tables, eagerly snatching at pastries and savories.

Halvar edged backward out of the overheated room. He paused at the bottom of the stairs. The snow had stopped, the wind had died down. The stars could be seen, surrounding the full moon in a cold, crisp sky.

It's Yule, Halvar thought. *The Long Night.*

He crossed the courtyard, slipped out the gate, and made his way back to the Mermaid Taberna. Tonight, he would celebrate with his own people, with good Danic ale and pickled herring. Tomorrow he would deal with the repercussions of Girard's murder.

He would call on the messenger who lodged with Prester Nicodemus and find out what Girard had really been doing in Manatas. He would have Leon translate the mysterious journal. He would send Locals over to the Long Island to rescue any of Captain Girard's papers that survived the wreck.

But tonight, he would celebrate Yule!

Chapter 26

TWO DAYS LATER, HALVAR FACED HIS THREE tenentes once again. The office was warm, thanks to the brazier. Selim, back in everyday padded coat and small turban, was seated in her place, notebook and ink at the ready.

"Firebrand, what do you hear from the Long Island? What happened to the round ship that went aground?"

"I sent Seulemon there yesterday as soon as the snow stopped and the water was calm enough for canoes. He came back today to report the woman Charlotte Summersby came off the wreck of the round boat alive. She was taken in charge by some Bretains who have a settlement they call Brook-line. As far as Seulemon can tell, she is well, but there is some question as to what to do with her.

"She will not clean or even tend the children, but she can sew well enough, and has been set to mending clothes. She complains about everything—the food, the company, even the clothes they have found for her to wear. They are Pure Sect on the Long Island, and disapprove of her finery. They will not let her wear the clothing she brought with her."

Halvar grinned under his mustache.

"I suppose the best way to shut her up will be to get her back here and let her husband see to her."

Flores sniggered. "He won't like that."

"That's his problem, not mine. More important, what of the contents of that ship? The maps and charts from the captain's cabin? Did the Bretain rescuers get those off before the ship sent under?"

Firebrand looked blank.

"Were they important? All those bits of paper?"

"Thor's Hammer! In the right hands, those maps and charts could mean life and death…or a fortune for the one who had them. When Seulemon goes back to fetch Milady, make sure he brings them with him."

"As you wish, Capitán."

"Tenente Flores, what have you heard from Emir Achmet and his Scavengers? Are they satisfied that Ibo has been avenged?"

Flores looked smug.

"As you suggested, I set the Scavengers to work clearing the snow from the streets. Emir Achmet was pleased to accept the extra payment on their behalf."

"And I'm sure he'll see that his people are fed and kept warm."

"With what they salvage from the woodpiles that others have collected." Flores grunted. "Ibo will have to wait until spring thaw, but the men who were hired to row Milord and his minion saw what happened— how the old woman fell into the bay—and they're satisfied that Ilha works in mysterious ways. No more problems with them, Capitán. At least, not for now."

Halvar turned to the third man standing in front of him.

"Tenente Donal, how go the preparations for Nativity in Green Village?"

"Well. Very well, Capitán. We've decided to combine the Yehudit mock fight with a kick-the-bladder bout of our own, the Green Village lads against a team from the madrassa. You are welcome to come and watch. It should be a good match."

"But not to take part," Halvar warned. "My days of kick-the-bladder are behind me."

"And what of Milord?" Flores asked. "What do we do with him?"

"Sultan Petrus will let him stay in the house they already occupy, unless he can make other arrangements with one of the owners of the Afrikan villas near the town wall. Edgar Norris and Andres Devallon are in his pay and stay with him. If they make trouble, we will deal with it, but as long as they don't, we let them go their own way."

"I'll have my men keep an eye on them anyway," Flores promised. "I don't like that Devallon."

"Nor do I," Halvar said. "But until he breaks the law, he's free to roam Manatas as he will." He rubbed his nose. "One more thing, Tenente Flores. I want you to take Zoltan and Fergus off the waterfront and post them at the souk."

"At the souk? Why? They know the waterfront—they live there," Flores protested. "And there's no good pickings at the souk."

"Just so." Halvar said. "Firebrand, I want *your* watchmen to patrol the waterfront. Flores, keep your men at the souk, on the Broad Way, and around the Rabat. Donal, your people are best kept in Green Village, but station them at either end of the town wall to keep watch there, too. Selim, write this down, see that every man knows where he's posted.

"And that's all for now," he said. "To your posts, Guardsmen. There's work to be done! Go to it!"

END

Author's Note

The song "Nova Mundum" in Chapter 17 should be sung to the tune of the Norwegian folk song "Oleanna."

GLOSSARY

AL-ANDALUS	Spain
AL-LARGATO	Alligator
ALGONKIN	Algonquin/Lenape Indians
ARABI	Arabic
ARAGHOUN	Raccoon
BATATAS	Potatoes
BRETAINS	British
CHESU	Jesus
CRUX	Cross
CORDUVA	Cordova
DANE-MARCH	Germany
DANES	The Germanic people (includes Denmark)
DANIC	Germanic language (written in Rune characters)
EAST CHANNEL	East River

GLOSSARY

END-OF-FAST	Eid Al-Fitr; Festival marking the end of Ramadan
ERSE	Gaelic language (written in Ogham characters)
ERSE RITE	Celtic Christianity as practiced in Northern Europe
ESCOUASH	Squash
FERIA	Commercial gathering/fair
FESTIVAL OF LIGHTS	Hanukkah
FRANCHEN	Language of Franchenland (written in Roman characters); a native of Franchenland
FRANCHENLAND	France
FRATER	General term for a Kristo cleric
FRATERY	Monastery

GLOSSARY

GREAT RIVER	Hudson River
HAMMAM	Communal bath
HEMP	Cannabis, Marijuana
HOLY BOOK	The Bible or the Qran, depending on who is speaking
HOLY MEAL	Mass
ILHA	Allah
ISLIM	Islam
KICK-THE-BLADDER	Football
KRISTO	Christian
KUTTON	Cotton
KIBBICK	Quebec
LOCALS	Native Americans
MACASSIN	Moccasin
MADRASSAH	School/university
MAHAK	Mohawk/Iroquois

GLOSSARY

MAIZ	Corn
MANATAS	Manhattan Island
MOKKA	Coffee
MOTHER MARA	Virgin Mary
MUNSI	Native trade language (unwritten)
MUSKAT	Mosque
NATIVITY	Christmas
NGUBA	"Goobers," peanuts
NOVA MUNDUM	"New World," North America
OLD GRECO	Ancient Greece
OLD ROUMI	Ancient Rome, Ancient Romans
OPASSOM	Opossum
OROPA	Europe, excluding Al-Andalus
PARIGI	Paris

GLOSSARY

PATRI NOSTRI	"Our Father"/Lord's Prayer
PISTOIA	Pistol
POWHATAN	Native Name For Terra Mara – Maryland
RABAT	Fortress
RHUM	Rum
ROUMI RITE	Christianity as practiced south of the Alps, centered in Rome
ROUND ISLAND	Staten Island
SALAAMABAD	Philadelphia
SAVANA PORT	Savannah, Ga.
SEKONK	Skunk
SEQUANOK	Pennsylvania
SOUK	Marketplace
STUDY HOUSE	Synagogue
TABAC	Tobacco

GLOSSARY

"Take the Water"	Be Baptized
The Pizzle	Florida
The Prophet	Mohammad
The Redeemer	Jesus
Three Old Women	Norns, Fates
Wamus	A deerskin shirt with a fringed yoke and sleeves
West Caster	Westchester / New England
wumpum	Wampum; Colored shells used as medium of exchange for small purchases
Yehudit	Jews / Jewish

About The Author

ROBERTA ROGOW wanted to tell stories from the moment she could hold a pencil, and to sing before she could walk. After a brief career as a professional chorister, coffee-house singer, and actress, she combined her love of literature with her love of music during a 37-year career as a children's librarian in New Jersey, where she could promote literacy and entertain youngsters.

In her spare time, Roberta wrote stories for fanzines incorporating historical characters into fictional situations. This led to paid publication, beginning with a story in the shared-universe anthology *Merovingen Nights*, edited by C.J. Cherryh, in 1987.

Since then, Roberta has written four mystery novels in which the Reverend. Mr. Charles Lutwidge Dodgson (Lewis Carroll) teams up with young Dr. Arthur Conan Doyle to solve crimes, and three set in post-Civil War New York City, where a team of waterfront lawyers take on cases that no one else will touch.

Now her love of history has turned in another direction with the Saga of Halvar, set in an alternate universe on what is almost, but not quite, Manhattan Island.

Roberta is a widow. She has two daughters: Miriam Ann Rogow, a travel agent living in San Francisco, who has written the Marti Hirsch mysteries, and Louise Katherine Howard, a computer programmer, who lives near Washington DC

About The Artist

Born in Chicago, *WILLIAM NEAGLE* graduated from the University of Tennessee with a BFA. Having done work for the US Department of Energy and other companies, his work has been distributed worldwide. He has done book covers for the writing team of Joreid McFate and for his own novel, *Catching the Ghost*. He resides in North Carolina with his wife and two children.

www.ingramcontent.com/pod-product-compliance
Lightning Source LLC
Chambersburg PA
CBHW031952240626
47153CB00003B/955